# DIRTY LAUNDRY

A J.J. GRAVES MYSTERY (BOOK 6)

LILIANA HART

A J.J. GRAVES MYSTERY

# DIRTY LAUNDRY

NEW YORK TIMES BESTSELLING AUTHOR

LILIANA HART

Published by 7th Press

*To Scott- because the conversation JJ and Jack have about where to eat might be a true story. And also because I love it when you give me a high five and tell me "good game."*

*Also to Ava, Ellie, Max, Jamie, and Graham- because I love you, even though it takes me twice as long to get my word count done for the day when you're home from school.*

# ACKNOWLEDGMENTS

A huge thanks to the readers who have been so patient while waiting for JJ and Jack's next adventure. I have the BEST readers, and I adore all of you.

A big thanks to Lyndsey Lewellen for always doing amazing covers. Thanks to my editor, Holly Atkinson, for cleaning up the messes. And thanks to Paul Salvette and Scott Silverii for taking care of the formatting.

Also a big thanks to Scott for being an amazing husband, partner, and cheerleader in life and business. I'm so blessed to have you, and I love you more every day.

**JJ Graves Mystery Series**

Dirty Little Secrets

A Dirty Shame

Dirty Rotten Scoundrel

Down and Dirty

Dirty Deeds

Dirty Laundry

Dirty Money

**The MacKenzies of Montana**

Dane's Return

Thomas's Vow

Riley's Sanctuary

Cooper's Promise

Grant's Christmas Wish

The MacKenzies Boxset

**MacKenzie Security Series**

Seduction and Sapphires

Shadows and Silk

Secrets and Satin

Sins and Scarlet Lace

Sizzle

Crave

Scorch

MacKenzie Security Omnibus 1

MacKenzie Security Omnibus 2

**Lawmen of Surrender (MacKenzies-1001 Dark Nights)**

1001 Dark Nights: Captured in Surrender

1001 Dark Nights: The Promise of Surrender

1001 Dark Nights: Sweet Surrender

1001 Dark Nights: Dawn of Surrender

**The MacKenzie World** (read in any order)

Trouble Maker

Bullet Proof

Deep Trouble

Delta Rescue

Desire and Ice

Rush

Spies and Stilettos

Wicked Hot

Hot Witness

Avenged

Never Surrender

**Addison Holmes Mystery Series**

Whiskey Rebellion

Whiskey Sour

Whiskey For Breakfast

Whiskey, You're The Devil

Whiskey on the Rocks

Whiskey Tango Foxtrot

Whiskey and Gunpowder

**The Gravediggers**

The Darkest Corner

Gone to Dust

Say No More

**Stand Alone Titles**

Breath of Fire

Kill Shot

Catch Me If You Can

All About Eve
Paradise Disguised
Island Home
The Witching Hour

**Books by Liliana Hart and Scott Silverii**
**The Harley and Davidson Mystery Series**
The Farmer's Slaughter
A Tisket a Casket
I Saw Mommy Killing Santa Claus
Get Your Murder Running
Deceased and Desist
Malice In Wonderland
Tequila Mockingbird
Gone With the Sin

# PROLOGUE

Yellow linen curtains billowed gently against the open windows of the little frame house. It was too early in the summer to turn on the air conditioner, and her fixed income appreciated the cool, breezy evenings that allowed her to stay comfortable during the night.

As far as safety was concerned, no one worried much about locking their doors or shutting their windows in Bloody Mary. The town was almost as safe as it had been sixty years before, when she'd moved there as a young bride.

Oh, how she missed her sweet Henry. He'd been gone now longer than they'd been married, and her memories of him were as a young man with an easy smile and lines at the corners of his eyes when he laughed. He was always laughing. They'd had twenty-two years together before his heart had given out.

They'd never been blessed with children, and she'd never had the heart to marry another, though she'd barely been forty when she'd found herself in widow's black. But she'd had a good life—a full life—filled with friends and community. And she'd been content to stay in the little house she and Henry had shared.

She'd filled the days since his death tending the bakery that she'd opened with his insurance money, providing sweets and baked goods to the whole county. She was proud to say that *Rosie's Sweet Shop* had become quite a hangout for Virginians through the years. She'd run it as long as she could before arthritis and age had caught up with her.

But age had only stopped her business, not her passion, and she still baked daily, handing out treats to anyone who looked like they could use a pick-me-up. The children on the street especially liked to come by after school for lemonade and cookies.

Yes, her life had been long and full, but there were days she ached to see her Henry again.

She sighed and reached down to pet the soft fur of the cat twining between her legs.

"Isn't that right, Andromeda?" she said, smiling as the cat purred back at her. "I only hope these wrinkles go away before he sees me again. I doubt he'd recognize me otherwise."

Jealous of the attention Andromeda was getting, Nicodemus and Juliet jumped down from the couch where they'd been watching a rerun of *Entertainment Tonight*, since television programming was rather limited at five in the morning, and they fought for the space between her feet.

The timer dinged from the kitchen and she pushed back the

chair at the little desk she'd been sitting at and closed the lid on her laptop. All her best work was done in the early morning hours, and she hadn't been able to break the habit of waking early to start her day with the sweet scents coming from her kitchen.

She pushed open the swinging door that led into the kitchen, the cats weaving around her feet, and took the yellow oven mitts from the counter. Her kitchen had always been cheerful and sunny—the bright yellow splashes of color making it seem more like daylight while the sky was still dark.

A cat meowed, and she glanced toward the ancient white Persian that was curled on the bench seat next to the big square window that looked out over her flowers. The only light came from the moon. She'd meant to replace the bulb on her back porch light, but it kept slipping her mind.

The fluffy white cat meowed again, but didn't move from his place on the bench.

"You always wake up when it's time to eat, right Charlemagne? Age hasn't affected your nose. Don't worry, you lazy boy. I'll bring you a plate." At fifteen, Charlemagne deserved a little pampering.

The cinnamon rolls had risen beautifully, and she set them on top of the stove so she could ice them. People always asked what made her icing taste so good, but she'd never told a soul. The recipe was her secret. She could *always* keep a secret.

She hummed Billie Holliday while she iced the cinnamon rolls and smiled at the scratches that came from the other side of the door. It swung back and forth a couple of times before there was enough room for Silas and Seamus—gray tabby brothers she'd found abandoned behind the Dollar Store dumpster—to slip through.

"Just in time, boys," she said. "Like clockwork. But you know they need to cool for a few minutes. Don't get greedy thinking you're going to jump up here and get a head start."

She covered the tray with a dish towel and put the empty icing bowl in the sink. The days of having someone wash her dishes while she did nothing but bake were long gone, and she filled the bowl with hot water and decided to let it wait a bit. She still had some work to do.

Her apron was tied around her dressing gown. She shucked it off and hung it on the hook on the back of the door as she pushed her way through to the living room, this time with only Juliet at her feet. Poor girl had never been the sharpest knife in the drawer.

The laptop was gone from the desk, and she stared at the empty space blankly for a minute or two, trying to remember what she'd done with the thing. She'd gotten quite good with computers over the years, doing her books and recipes, among other things, with ease. She was sure she'd left it right there on the desk. But maybe…

A crash came from the bedroom, glass shattered, and she gasped and spun toward the bedroom door, a hand to her heaving chest. And then she let out a twinkle of a laugh as a streak of orange slithered around the doorjamb and hid under the couch.

"Heavens, Lucille," she said. "You near scared me to death. And what have you broken? I told you to stay off my dresser, you naughty thing."

She shuffled into the bedroom, her house slippers scraping against the hardwood floors, and made her way to the lamp on her nightstand. The moonlight cast a triangle of silvery light on the floor and the corner of her bed.

Her hand searched for the dangling chain of the lamp, and she'd just gotten hold of it when she saw a shadow pass across the triangle of light and rush straight toward her.

There was no time to do more than whimper as something crashed against the side of her head. Then there was nothing but blackness.

# 1

## The King George Tattler

*My loyal readers:*

*What a week it's been! I think it's true what they say about extreme temperatures. Surely the only explanation for the behavior of some of King George County's finest is due to the heat wave. Tempers are short and poor life choices are at an all-time high. That's good news for me and great news for you, as you're the ones paying the subscription fee for such juicy gossip.*

*I've got eyewitness reports that say there was quite a ruckus at King George Hospital this week. Dr. and Mrs. Trevor Sloane welcomed a bouncing baby boy. Unfortunately, Baby Boy Sloane has a remarkable resemblance to Rafael Ortega, who has been gardening more than the Sloane's front yard, if you get my meaning. It's said the screams of outrage could be heard through the whole hospital, and Dr. Sloane had to be escorted from the premises. There's more to this story, but you'll have to wait for next week's edition.*

*Our deepest sympathies here at the Tattler go out to Mayor Walsh in Nottingham. I've heard through the grapevine that he'd planned to put his hat in the ring for the next gubernatorial election, but with the early stages of Parkinson's disease setting in, who knows if that dream will become a reality.*

*Rumor also has it that King George's very own A-lister, Cherise Dupree, has taken up residence at her mother's house for the summer after a nasty divorce and whisperings of financial mismanagement. Of course, those of you who grew up here during a certain era know that her name wasn't always Cherise Dupree, but mum's the word on that little secret. I can't do all the work for you, now can I?*

*Oh...this is a doozy. Hearts broke across the state of Virginia when our own Sheriff Lawson decided to take himself off the most eligible bachelor list last month. And to a most unlikely candidate, as county coroner JJ Graves is hardly the woman any of us would have matched him with. Especially since her parents are known felons. Ahh...but they say love is blind, after all.*

*Or is it?*

*I saw with my very own eyes a certain sheriff's vehicle parked in the alleyway behind the strip mall on Catherine of Aragon just past three in the morning. Let's just say that the vehicle was rocking. You all know the rest of the saying. And in my experience, though you know I'd never make assumptions, shenanigans like that typically don't happen between married couples.*

*There's no need to sneak about when one has that shiny gold band around the finger, unless a certain someone is sneaking about with someone other than his wife. Only time will tell if the sheriff's marriage is on the rocks. I know there are plenty of women interested in him becoming a free agent once again. Of course, who knows if this will hurt his chances of reelection come November. Only time will tell...*

"That vile, horrible bit—" I started to say before I remembered I was trying not to swear so much.

"Good catch," Vaughn said, not looking up from the laptop where he'd been reading aloud. "Your quarter jar is getting pretty full."

I gave him a narrowed look and went back to the task of refilling my oversized coffee mug that warned others to approach with caution. I added extra cream and sugar and prayed this cup would be the one that had me on full alert. I'm a slow starter in the mornings, so I generally give myself a good two hours to acclimate before I allow myself to join the general population. It's safer for everyone that way.

My name is JJ Graves, and I had good reason to add a few extra quarters into my swear jar. According to the KGT—short for *King George Tattler*—my month-long marriage was on the brink of disaster. It didn't matter that Madam Scandal, who'd brought both terror and titillation into the lives of the residents of King George County, Virginia for months now, was correct about seeing Jack's truck in the alley behind the strip mall. She'd also been right about what had been happening *inside* the truck.

I wanted to give Madam Scandal credit where credit was due. She certainly got around, and her accuracy level was impressive. And terrifying. I could see where she'd assume it was someone besides me in the car with Jack. We had no excuse for our behavior other than we'd been stuck working a late-night suicide and we'd had a lot of pent up energy to dispose of on the way home. At least that's the justification I'm most comfortable with.

It's not as easy to do spontaneous, irresponsible things like that once you're in your thirties. Jack was still limping from where he'd twisted his knee, and I'd done something to my hip. Which is depressing, because I'm at the age where I can say things like, "I've done something to my hip."

I'll admit, I've enjoyed marriage much more than I ever thought possible. Of course, I only had my parents to look to as an example, so I didn't really have a lot of high expectations going in. But Jack was my best friend, and he filled a place in me that had been empty for far too long.

"Top me off, would you?" Vaughn asked, holding out his cup.

"You find this entertaining, don't you?"

"If I say yes, will you still give me coffee?"

I sighed and brought the pot to where he'd been sitting on the barstool beside me, filling his cup. Vaughn took it black, no sugar.

The men in my life took care of their bodies. I, on the other hand, was living on the borrowed time of good genetics and metabolism, as I had the eating habits of a college freshman. Sugar and gluten were two of my favorite ingredients.

As someone who gets an intimate look at the body after one dies, you'd think I'd be more cautious about such things. I've seen the damage that unhealthy lifestyles cause on the organs. But one thing I know with certainty is that we'll all eventually end up six feet under. There's no escaping death, so I might as well enjoy life.

"Keep reading," I said. "Who's next?"

"You and Jack were the last," he said. "I'd say she did a pretty good job this week. She ruined Joe Walsh's chances of running for governor and she essentially put Jack back on the open market."

I rolled my eyes. "I'm not sure the women here ever considered him *off* the market. It amazes me how little the sight of a wedding ring seems to matter to some of these women."

"Nothing but harlots," Vaughn agreed sympathetically. "And Jack's gotten good at deflecting unwanted advances over the years. You know, there was a time when I actually thought that's what he majored in at college."

I would've laughed, but I could see how the assumption could be made. Jack oozed alpha sex appeal. It was just part of his makeup.

Vaughn was dressed for work in summer linen pants and a pressed white button-down shirt that was open at the collar. He skimmed just over six feet, but he had the kind of posture that made him seem taller, probably from years of playing the piano. He had black hair and a goatee, and his nails were clean and well-manicured. His shoes cost more than everything in my closet combined.

Much like Jack, Vaughn came from a long line of tobacco farmers, though Vaughn's father hadn't had the golden touch like John Lawson. And then Mr. Raines had had a heart attack in the middle of his fields and died, leaving the family rich in heritage but destitute in cash.

Vaughn had been a semester away from graduating college, but he'd packed up and come home to take care of things. He'd swallowed his pride and taken a loan from Jack's father, liquidated items in the house and barns before the bank foreclosed on them, paid off creditors, and moved his mother into a small home in a retirement community that she constantly complained about.

Vaughn's passion was antiquities, and he had an eye for quality. But he knew selling antiques in the warehouse he'd bought at auction wouldn't provide for stable living. He figured the thing people cared about the most in life was themselves, so in the other half of the warehouse he'd opened up a health and vitamin supercenter. It was the only one in King George County and Vaughn had quickly become a success.

Next to Jack, Vaughn was my best friend in the world. A few months back, his lover had been brutally murdered and he was still grieving the loss. But I was starting to see glimpses of the man he'd been before the tragedy. There was still a shadow in his eyes that I wasn't sure time would ever heal. I couldn't imagine living in a world without Jack. That kind of love was rare. And I hated that Vaughn would have that missing piece for the rest of his life.

He looked at his watch. "I've got to open the store soon."

"Sure you don't want to get breakfast?" I asked.

"No, some of us don't keep mortician's hours."

"Death is down this month," I said, shrugging. "It'll pick back up at the end of July and August. The heat wipes out a lot of seniors."

"That's fascinating and horrible," he said, staring at me in shock. "But mostly horrible. You're much too casual about death."

"Never," I said. "But it's something I've learned to accept. Something that happens to everyone. And there's rarely dignity in death. It's my job to give it back to them. But if I don't keep a sense of humor, I'll go crazy."

I opened the pantry and grabbed a box of Pop Tarts. "Who do you think she is?" I asked, changing the subject. Even when I was at my most awake, I didn't like to dwell too much on the seriousness of death. It was too easy to get lost in the darkness and not find the way back out.

"What?" he asked. "Who?"

I raised my brows and pointed to the laptop. "The woman, of course. Who do you think she is?"

"I haven't given it much thought," he said, looking into his coffee.

"Liar." I pulled the barstool close to him and took a seat. "You've come here every Thursday for the past five months so we can read the salacious gossip of people we've known our whole lives, and you're telling me you haven't thought of it? I call bullhockies."

"Bullhockies?"

"I'm out of quarters," I said, shrugging. "I'll have to stop by the bank later for emergencies."

The corner of Vaughn's mouth twitched. "That's pathetic. Maybe you need to bump it up to a dollar. I'm sure you'll stop swearing in no time."

"Maybe you need to mind your own beeswax," I said, eyes narrowed.

He barked out a laugh at that.

"You mark my words," I said. "This woman is asking for trouble. How long do you think she can really keep her identity a secret? I guarantee you and I both know her. She might even live in Bloody Mary. No one has secrets in Bloody Mary."

I opened the shiny packaging of the Pop Tart and bit into it cold while Vaughn stared at me in horror.

"I can't believe you're putting that into your body," he said. "The preservatives alone…"

"I figure I have to keep eating preservatives at this point," I said. "If I start introducing good stuff into my body, it'll probably go into shock and I'll die. Then you'll all be very sad, and all those women will eat Jack alive the second they find out he's single again. He'll have to put himself into Witness Protection."

"First of all, that's ridiculous. Jack would never let himself be eaten alive."

I narrowed my eyes. "I like how you didn't agree with me about being sad because I'm dead."

He ignored me. "And second of all, how are you a doctor? That's the most insane logic I've ever heard. I hope that's not the kind of advice you'd give patients."

"All of my patients are dead," I said. "They're great listeners, but don't really take my advice all that often. But if it makes you feel better, I'll eat it after you've gone so you don't have to worry."

"Are you taking those fruit and veggie pills from the store I brought you?" he asked.

"Every day," I lied. "I'm healthy as a horse. Promise."

"Good," he said. "Now if I can just keep the two of you out of the back seats of cars in the middle of the night, I'll feel as if I've succeeded as a parent."

I rolled my eyes. "Don't be so judgmental. It could be you who shows up in next week's edition. None of us are safe. We need to find out who this woman is. It'd be a service to the community."

"As it happens," he said, "I agree with you. We should make a list of everyone she's ever outed. We could find out their address and put pins in a map, and then see where the central location is."

I raised my brows in surprise. "I feel like you've given this a lot of thought, Nancy Drew. Are you sure you need me?"

"Of course," he said, slapping me on the back. "Jack has that big map of the county in his office and unlimited police resources. I bet we'll have her outed by the end of the week."

"If we out her," I said, "how are we going to find out all the gossip? Maybe she's the one doing a service for the community. Think of all the bad things we've learned about people. She's really opened our eyes. She even got an investigation opened on Ronnie Dowel for soliciting minors. A lot of people see her as a hero."

"The police were already investigating Ronnie," Vaughn said. "Jack told us that. And good riddance to him. But this woman is stirring up trouble all over the place. No one trusts each other anymore. And you have to wonder just how accurate all her stories are. Look at the insinuations she posed just on the story of you and Jack."

"Madam Scandal reports what she sees," I said, shrugging. "How was she supposed to know it was me in the back of Jack's unit in that alleyway? Unless she was looking in the window, of course."

He stared at me reproachfully, and I felt the heat creeping up my neck. "Y'all are too old to be pulling stunts like that. Don't think I haven't noticed Jack's been limping all week."

"It's just an old injury acting up," I said, pressing my lips together and avoiding eye contact.

"Uh huh," he said. "I'm just saying this woman has already crossed lines. She's got access to private information that no one should have. Medical information. Financial information. What if she printed information about your parents that no one else had access to?"

That thought made my blood run cold. Up until a few months ago, I thought my parents had been hauling coal in hell for the things they'd done on earth. They'd been using the family funeral home to smuggle all kinds of contraband into the country. They'd contracted with the government to bring home soldiers who'd died overseas, only to contract with another agency across the water to use the bodies as storage facilities for whatever they wanted to bring into the United States. There'd been a lot of money involved and a lot of danger. I didn't know a fraction of what had really happened, but as soon as my parents' car ran over that cliff, the FBI had been on me, and everything that had been left to me, like white on rice.

I'd found all of this information out by accident, stumbling across a bunker full of boxes and a dead body my father had left there to rot. Part of me wished I'd never found those boxes. Inside them had been truths I hadn't wanted to know. Maybe there are some people out there who want the truth, no matter the cost, but after what I'd been through, I wasn't sure I was one of those people anymore. Sometimes the truth is kept secret to protect others. And sometimes the truth is so horrific that once it's known, life can never be the same.

The first box I'd gone through had been full of nothing but papers and information about me. The *real* me. I tried to find some comfort in the fact that *their* blood didn't really run through my veins, but it wasn't much comfort at all. My parents had been some kind of double agents, but the facts were murky at best. My mother had been shot in France while on a mission and had lost the baby she'd been carrying. I'd been the substitute. Stolen from other parents. Parents who probably had ethics and morals and didn't hide contraband in dead bodies. In the other boxes had been stacks of cash, IDs, and flash drives.

I'd thought briefly about destroying all of it. The records, the cash...*everything*. It seemed a simple solution to a complicated problem. But I've learned in my lifetime that the problems that seem to plague me never have a simple solution. Burning it all would have been simple if my parents had really died in a car crash, their bodies so unrecognizable that they'd had to be identified by the dental records.

But they hadn't died in that crash. It had been their escape when the life they'd chosen to live went south. The boxes of cash and IDs and information had been their insurance policy and a way to start over. But I'd gotten in the way, as it seemed I always had, and my father had shown up to collect what I'd discovered. It hadn't exactly been a joyous reunion. But he'd told me to give him a chance to explain and that everything wasn't as it seemed. And then he'd stolen every box and shred of evidence from the safe in our home without batting an eyelash.

Jack and I hadn't seen him since, and no one else knew he was alive. But I watched over my shoulder, waiting for him to come back, felt his eyes on me from time to time. I'd given Jack permission to send a few of the flash drives to a trusted friend to see what was on them. Malachi Graves wasn't the kind of man to leave loose ends. Even if the loose end was his daughter.

"Maybe you're right," I said, blowing out a breath. "Shutting her down is the best thing we can do. For the community."

Vaughn and I knuckle bumped and he pulled out a pad and pen from the briefcase he'd sat on the island.

"It always makes me nervous when the two of you have your heads together like that," Jack said from behind us.

Vaughn and I both jumped guiltily and turned to look at him. He'd left the house just after six that morning, and I vaguely remembered him giving me a kiss and setting a cup of coffee on the bedside table before he'd left for work. I wasn't a morning person. Jack, on the other hand, was alert and annoyingly pleasant in the mornings.

"What are you doing home?" I asked.

"The better question is, why aren't you at work? I've been calling for almost twenty minutes."

"Oh," I said, glancing at my phone that was still plugged into the charger. "I must have it on silent. It hasn't rung."

There was a moment of awkward silence as Jack stood there and stared at us, assessing us with those cop eyes. King George County wasn't huge by city standards. It was divided into four towns—King George Proper and Bloody Mary to the north, and Nottingham and Newcastle to the south. Jack had been the youngest sheriff ever elected, and he'd done a hell of a job with little resources and a community that was more than set in their ways.

It was an agricultural community for the most part. The rich were *really* rich and the poor were *really* poor. It wasn't easy to find the middle class, though it existed in certain pockets that were more affordable to live in. But Jack managed to relate to everyone and he'd been approached more than once about taking up a higher political office.

He was the kind of man that everyone might not like, but

respected. He'd been a SWAT cop in DC for a handful of years and gotten invaluable experience on the job. Then he'd been shot three times in the line of duty and lost some good friends in the same SWAT raid. That's when he'd decided to move home to Bloody Mary.

The things that had happened in that bank—the lies, the betrayals, and the ultimate sacrifices that had been made—had changed something in Jack forever. He was healing from those wounds, but I still caught glimpses of pain I feared might never come to the surface.

Where Vaughn was GQ polished with his expensive clothes and shoes, Jack looked like a working man, even though he was one of the wealthiest men in the state. A fact that still made me uncomfortable.

He wore jeans and a denim work shirt that had the sleeves rolled up to just below his elbows. His duty belt was cinched around a trim waist, as much a part of him as one of his limbs, and his badge was pinned above his breast pocket. His dark hair was buzzed close to the scalp and he already showed signs of a day's worth of stubble, even though I knew he'd shaved that morning. The scar that slashed through his eyebrow was white, indicating the level of his annoyance.

I caught myself staring and felt the slow flush of desire heat my skin. Sex appeal. He had it in spades. And it was all for me.

"It's Thursday," I finally managed to get out.

"Yes," he said. "And tomorrow is Friday." He went to the kitchen cabinet and grabbed a to-go cup, then took my freshly poured mug and transferred the contents to the new cup. Never a good sign.

"I don't go into the funeral home until ten on Thursdays unless there's a body." I was glad I'd already showered and dressed for the day so I didn't look like a complete slug-a-bug.

"Right," Jack said. "The *King George Tattler* comes out on Thursdays. Anything good today?"

"I've got to take off," Vaughn said, not wanting to be the one to break the news. "I've got to open the store. But I'm free tomorrow night, Jaye. Text me your schedule. I'm off at five."

"Do I want to know?" Jack grabbed my cell phone, handed it to me, then put the to-go mug in my other hand. Apparently, I was going somewhere in a hurry, and considering my profession, it was probably a good call that I'd dressed in old jeans and a black sleeveless tee. I was hell on clothes, either ruining them with questionable stains or smells that never washed out.

"We're going to use your numerous police resources to discover the identity of Madam Scandal," Vaughn said, grinning.

"The taxpayers will love that," Jack said dryly.

"I'll buy the pizza to even things out. Believe me, after you read today's episode, you're going to want to catch her as much as we do."

Jack sighed, reading between the lines. "Lovely."

"Catch you guys later," Vaughn said, hitching the strap of

his briefcase over his shoulder and giving us an off-handed wave goodbye.

"I'm going to assume there's a body that's in need of my attention," I said as the front door closed.

"The call came in early this morning," he said.

"Homicide?" I asked.

"We'll treat it as such until you can rule it out," he said vaguely. "But you're probably going to want to wear two coveralls. And maybe a hazmat suit. It's messy."

I blew out a sigh. I hated the messy ones.

# 2

MARRIAGE HAD SETTLED ME IN A WAY I'D NEVER THOUGHT possible.

I'd spent my entire life displaced—not belonging—to my family or community. I always seemed to be on the outside looking in. There was something about growing up in a small town that was hard to explain to people who had never experienced it. You either belonged or you didn't. You were either someone or you weren't. And those things were usually determined before birth, depending on who your parents were.

My parents had always been so absorbed in themselves there hadn't been much time for anything else. For four generations, my family had been a part of Bloody Mary. They'd owned a business and raised their children. But I'm not sure anyone could say they were a part of the community on more than a surface level. Close friends weren't possible when living a life of deception.

I found it ironic that my home with Jack—a place I finally

felt I belonged—was on the same street as the home I'd grown up in—a place I'd never belonged. The same street, but worlds apart. But that place was in the past, at the end of a long stretch of Heresy Road. It was someone else's albatross now.

My home with Jack was two miles in the opposite direction, down a two-lane country road that was a mixture of gravel and potholes and wound through towering trees. If you rolled down the windows in the car, you could hear the rush of the Potomac River. And at the end of that two-mile stretch, tucked back in the trees on the edge of a cliff, was my paradise. The log cabin structure that Jack had built had become ours.

I loaded my medical bag and a few extras into the back of Jack's unit, and we headed to the scene. He still hadn't given me any information, and I wondered if it was intentional so I could see it with fresh eyes, or if he just couldn't bring himself to tell me about it yet.

The other thing about living in a small town was that in our line of work, you tended to know the victim.

"If you'll give me the address, I'll have one of the interns meet us with the Suburban so we can transport the body," I said to break the silence.

"There's plenty of time for that," he said, tapping his index finger against the steering wheel. "The victim is Rosalyn McGowen."

"What?" I turned to face him, the seatbelt biting into my hip. "Damn."

When we were kids, Mrs. McGowen had given us cookies

and lemonade every day after school at the bakery. There was nothing that tasted better than those cookies. She was a Bloody Mary treasure.

"Quarter," Jack said out of habit.

"I'm out."

"I put extra for you in the cup holder."

"You can't fund my swear jar. That defeats the purpose."

"Emmy Lu gave me five dollars out of your petty cash drawer. You're funding it."

Emmy Lu Stout was my new receptionist. She was a Bloody Mary native and a dozen years or so older than I was. She'd married her high school sweetheart at eighteen and given birth to five boys before the age of twenty-five. And then when the youngest had graduated high school, her husband had decided to trade her in for a newer model and filed for divorce, leaving her with half the mortgage and bills, and nothing in the joint checking account.

She was just about the sweetest woman I'd ever met and cute as a button, like a middle-aged Gidget with crow's feet and thirty pounds heavier. I'd hired her on the spot. And I couldn't really blame her for giving Jack the money out of petty cash. He could pretty much charm anyone into doing what he wanted. And if charm didn't work, he had other methods, but he usually saved those for the criminals instead of law-abiding citizens.

"You keep your charms off my receptionist, Jack Lawson, or you're going to end up with a roll of quarters up your—"

"Uh, uh, uh," he said, mouth twitching. "I only got five dollars' worth. That temper is going to get you in trouble."

"I'm shaking in my boots," I said. "Let's focus on Mrs. McGowen. I'll deal with you later."

"Sounds kinky."

I couldn't stop the grin that wanted to spread across my face, so I ducked my head and dug around in my bag for a hair-band. My dark hair was getting to a length that was starting to get annoying. It normally swung just below my chin, long enough that I could pull it back out of my face. But I hadn't gotten a trim in months and it flirted with the top of my shoulders. I'd like to say it was because I've been so busy, but if I was honest, the real reason I hadn't gotten it cut was because Jack seemed to enjoy the longer length.

"Carl Planter found her this morning," Jack said. "He lives next door."

He turned onto Anne Boleyn, which was Bloody Mary's equivalent of a Main Street. It led directly to the Town Square, which was where the corners of all four cities in King George County met. Businesses had just opened for the day. Sidewalks were being swept and conversations were being had. A line went into the little coffee shop on the corner.

"Carl Planter," I said. The name sparked recognition. "I remember him from school. Didn't he get expelled for being a peeping Tom in the locker room?"

"That was always the rumor," Jack said. "Who knows for sure? It didn't help that he started homeschooling sophomore year. I heard his mom pulled him out because he was spending all his time in the bathroom masturbating to whatever he saw in the locker room instead of in class."

I curled my lip in disgust. "I didn't need to know that," I said.

Jack smiled. "Dickie saw him going into the shower once and said he had raw spots on his shaft because he did it so often."

"Yikes," I said. "I didn't even know he still lived in Bloody Mary. I thought he and his mom moved to Pittsburgh."

"She did," Jack said. "Would you want to be known as the mom of the boy who masturbated himself raw? I can't even imagine how that conversation went."

"I really appreciate you telling me all this," I said. "It'll make things much less awkward when we have to talk to him. I hope his blisters have healed."

"Maybe it's like playing the guitar. Maybe it just calluses over after time."

"Seriously, you've put way too much thought into this. I can honestly say that's something I've never seen in all my years as a doctor."

"There's always a first for everything. You can count on human nature for that."

Traffic was heavy as Anne Boleyn merged toward the Town Square and all the municipal buildings. Jack turned on his lights and sirens and watched the traffic part in front of us. He turned away from the Town Square and into a residential section of town.

"Anyway," Jack said, once he cleared the traffic. "Carl got worried when he hadn't seen Mrs. McGowen this week. She rarely goes a day without putting out cookies for the kids or taking someone something. He said just last Sunday she made loaves of banana bread for everyone on the street. He carried the basket for her."

"Poor thing," I said, heart heavy. Mrs. McGowen was one of the sweeter memories from my childhood. She'd always had a kind word and a little something extra for me. The older I got, the more I realized how many people in the community had taken up the slack for me where my parents had failed. Teachers, neighbors, parents of friends… They'd recognized the lost girl I was and given me what they could.

It was a heartening thought, and I realized I needed to look at my community with less cynicism. That tended to be my first response to everything. Jack's too. Which wasn't unusual considering our line of work. Everyone lied. Everyone had an angle.

I thought about Mrs. McGowen and felt a pang in my chest. "I guess it's comforting to think she's finally with her husband," I said. "She always said she was looking forward to the day she could see him again. It's amazing, though… She spent more years as a widow than she did married to him, but she never stopped loving him."

Jack smiled. "When we'd go to the bakery after school, she'd talk about him as if he were still alive. When she tried out new recipes or had decisions to make, he always got a say so."

"She lived a long life," I said. "She's got to be well past eighty. She knew my grandmother."

"Eighty-five and going strong, or so it seemed."

"It seemed?" I remembered what he'd said about the scene being messy. "What aren't you telling me that's going to make me hate my job today?"

"You never hate your job," he said. "But she had cats."

I winced. That wasn't good news. "How bad is it?"

"In our line of work, that's all relative. But if she had dogs, we'd be dealing with an entirely different situation. Cats have no loyalty."

"I'll be sure to put out the PSA."

"I had the guys contain the cats in the spare bedroom. It's about as contaminated a scene as you can get. Cheek lasted about ten seconds before he lost his breakfast in the bushes."

"Gotta love rookies."

Jack turned on his blinker when we got to the corner of Oleander and Foxglove, and I could see the emergency vehicles parked midway down the street. I could also see Floyd Parker's green SUV pulled along the sidewalk. He was casually talking to the neighbors who were huddled together in the street. Someone had given him a cup of coffee.

"I hate that man," I said, feeling my blood pressure spike automatically.

"Look at it this way," Jack said. "Ever since Madam

Scandal started publishing the *King George Tattler*, business at the *Gazette* has gone way down. Ernie Myers has been talking about downsizing the staff and going to digital only."

Ernie Myers was the owner of the *Gazette*. "That does make me feel better."

Floyd and I had a long, complicated history mostly made of bad decisions on each of our parts. I was working on being a forgiving person and looking to the future, but I'd be lying if I said I'd be upset if a truck fell on his head. I'd even do his funeral for free.

Foxglove Court was a cul-de-sac street of older homes with plenty of yard and lots of trees. It was the kind of street where the sidewalks were cracked and the lawns were well-manicured. Box shrubs lined the front of most houses and screened-in porches held rocking chairs and hanging plants. American flags were attached to eaves and waved proudly in the summer breeze. I noticed a couple of the houses had *Jack Lawson for Sheriff* signs in their yards.

The thought of the November election already had my guts knotting. I wasn't sure I was cut out to be a politician's wife, but I didn't really have a choice at this point. The county needed Jack and I was going to do everything in my power not to embarrass him.

I still worried if my parents' criminal past would hurt him when it was dragged up during election time. There was no doubt it *would* be dragged up. Floyd Parker at the *Gazette* would do everything he could to cost Jack the election.

"You fall asleep?" Jack asked, waving a hand in front of my face.

"Sorry, got lost in thought." And then I nodded toward the signs. "Looks like you have some supporters."

"Relax," he said, seeing my tension. "We're not here to win over constituents. We're here to do a job. I'm not worried about the election, and you shouldn't be either."

"Easy for you to say," I muttered under my breath.

I recognized most of the officers that were standing outside of the gray house with white trim. Officer Chen was stationed just outside the screen door on the steps, her uniform crisp and her hands folded in front of her. She was small in stature, but I wouldn't have tried to go through her. She'd been a transplant from Atlanta and had a lot more experience than most of the officers with the King George Sheriff's Office. I'd seen her take down a drunk man more than twice her size.

I'd saved myself some time by putting on my coveralls at the house, and I'd taken Jack's advice and put on two pair. I was never sure what I might have to kneel in. I grabbed my bag and slung my digital camera around my neck, and then followed Jack toward the front door. He was getting an update from Officer Chen.

I nodded to some of the neighbors and realized I didn't recognize most of them. It reminded me how quickly Bloody Mary was growing. Everyone wanted to move here from the city for better schools and lower cost of living, but the irony was the influx of people were making Bloody Mary lose the small-town feel.

I did see Carl Planter standing close to another man, comforting him, and they had the kind of stance that told me they were intimate partners. It was easy to see the groupings—families and close friends clung together—some weeping softly. Everyone knew Mrs. McGowen and she'd be missed. And Floyd Parker stood there like a poisonous toad.

I turned away from the onlookers and watched as Chen checked her notebook several times while she reported to Jack. She must have been the first officer on scene. Detectives Nash and Martinez were standing in the driveway, razzing Officer Cheek. Cheek was an unusual shade of green and his face was covered in sweat. He didn't look like it would take much to lose the rest of his breakfast.

"Good luck, Doc," Martinez called out. "I've got twenty riding that you won't barf. Do me proud."

"I appreciate the vote of confidence, Martinez," I said. "Just so you know, I've never barfed at a scene, but I hope you didn't make the bet with Nash. He still owes me twenty from the World Series."

"There was a budget shortage," Nash said. "Double or nothing next World Series. You'll get your money, Doc."

"Knocking up that girl at the bar doesn't count as a budget shortage, dumbass," Martinez said, laughing. "That's called child support. I told you she was nothing but trouble, but you never listen. Only thinking with your—"

I tuned out their good-natured ribbing and nodded to Officer Chen. There was sweat on her upper lip, but I wasn't sure if it was because of the heat that was already saturating the day or because of what she'd seen.

I climbed the three steps that led to the screen door of the porch, then stopped and put on blue booties over my sneakers. I handed Jack a pair as well and latex gloves, and then blew into mine before slipping them on with practiced ease.

"I got confirmation of the deed on the way back from the house. Residence legally belongs to Rosalyn Neeley McGowen, aged eighty-five as of last month. Home purchased in 1953 by Henry Herbert McGowen."

He held open the screen door for me and I walked onto a neat little porch with two rocking chairs. The screens that enclosed the porch looked fairly new. In fact, the whole outside of the house was in excellent upkeep, and I wondered if neighbors volunteered to help her out or if Mrs. McGowen had a regular handyman.

The front door was bright red and cheerful, but I could smell the stench of death that permeated from the space within. I could also hear what sounded like screams of torture. Jack opened the front door and I covered my ears.

"Good grief, what is that?" I yelled over the screeches. "It's awful."

"Cats," he said. "Animal control just pulled up." He closed the front door again to drown out the sounds.

I blew out a breath in relief and moved to the side so the two animal control officers could get through with cages. It certainly explained why Cheek was looking a little green around the gills. Cats were predators by nature. Beloved owner or not, the cats would only wait so long before their carnal nature took over and they decided to feast.

Jack was right. She should have had dogs.

A minute or two passed and one of the officers opened the front door and ran to the side of the house. Sounds of retching could barely be heard over the screeches. Jack pulled the door closed again to drown them out.

The other officers came back out, carrying two cages with a total of seven cats. The cats' hair was matted with blood and they were all spitting mad.

"Sorry, Burg," Jack said to the officer.

"No worries. I did two tours in Iraq. There's not a lot that fazes me." He held up one of the cages. "What should we do with the cats?"

"Take them to my lab," I told them. "We might have to swab them for particulates and check fecal matter for any remains."

"The interns are going to love that one," Jack said, the corner of his mouth twitching.

"I just got assigned new ones last week. I hope they have a stronger constitution than the last one they sent me. If that boy had fainted one more time in the lab, I was just going to leave him there."

Virginia Commonwealth University sent me interns every semester. I'd had a few decide they needed to choose a different career path after spending time doing what I do. We'd had some pretty interesting cases over the last several months, and my name was appearing frequently in the papers. I was starting to get business from all over the county now, and I was having trouble keeping up with everything. Which was the reason I'd hired a receptionist.

I texted Emmy Lu so she could get all hands on deck and arrange for the Suburban to be here for transport. I also let her know she needed to find a place for a bunch of angry, bloody cats.

"Man, I really wanted to have steak tonight for dinner," Jack said. "Seeing those cats is almost enough to make me change my mind."

"I won't tell anyone you're turning in your man card," I said. "But steak sounds good to me. I have a feeling lunch won't be happening today."

I'd been dealing with the dead long enough that nothing really bothered me anymore. It was easy to become desensitized to the horrors that can happen to the human body, but my humanity and compassion remained because I could see the affect death had on the living. Fortunately, I'd just gotten used to the smells.

"Does Mrs. McGowen have any family?" I asked Jack.

"None that I know of. She's been alone since her husband died. I don't ever recall her talking about any other family, but we'll see if anyone else has information."

I followed Jack through the front door and into a tiny entryway that opened into the living room. It was a shotgun style house, with the dining room and kitchen directly behind it, and a hallway to the left of the dining room.

"I worked a mass shooting in DC that looked a lot like this," Jack said.

It took a second for my brain to translate what my eyes were seeing.

"Holy sh…crap," I corrected. "It's amazing how much blood is in the human body."

"It's even more amazing how much of a mess seven cats can make in a tiny house. What does it say about me that the cat poop bothers me way more than the blood?"

"It means you're normal. But look on the bright side, you get to assign your officers to collect it all and bring it back to the lab."

He grimaced. "I'll put Nash in charge since he still owes you the twenty. You can call it even."

Jack's eyes started watering and he pinched the bridge of his nose. The ammonia in the cat urine was overwhelming. I pulled out two surgical masks from my bag. It wouldn't kill the smell completely, but it would let us do our job without passing out.

Under normal circumstances, the room would have been cheerful, and I imagined, tidy. There was one small yellow-striped couch and a denim blue La-Z-Boy in the living room. Yellow Priscillas hung at the windows and a small television was set up on a TV tray. There was a desk pushed against the wall and an upholstered chair beneath it in a floral print.

But this was far from normal circumstances. Blood smeared the walls, and there were outlines of perfect paw prints on the couch and chair. No surface was spared. There were droplets of blood on the ceiling, and I could only imagine how it had gotten up there. Where there wasn't blood there was feces, and the rugs and upholstery were saturated with urine. Just to complete the decoration, a light misting of cat hair covered everything. I already wanted to take a shower.

"How'd Carl discover the body?" I asked.

"Chen was first on scene and talked to Carl before she went in to look at the body. He told her Mrs. McGowen usually gets the mail at four o'clock every day. That's the same time he gets home from work, but he worked late on Monday so he missed her. On Tuesday and Wednesday, he said he was home like clockwork, but he didn't see her. He got worried and checked her mailbox this morning and saw it was full, so he gathered it up and went and knocked on the door. He has a key in case of emergencies and let himself in when she didn't answer, thinking she might have been sick or hurt. He took one look, closed the door, and called 9-1-1."

It sounded like Carl had handled things calmly and efficiently. I guess I'd expect that from a person who could rub themselves raw masturbating. Someone with that kind of dedication could get the job done.

"Stop thinking about it," Jack said.

"I can't," I confessed. "It's like staring at an ant pile after it's been kicked. I'll never be able to look at Carl the same."

I'd had little dealings with scavengers and human remains, but it happened from time to time. A body left too long in the woods or in the water would always have some animal marks. And I'd once seen a body that had been eaten by rats in the morgue of Augusta General. They'd even eaten bone, and the identity of the victim had been almost impossible to determine by normal means.

I tried not to pay too close attention to the interior of the house as we made our way toward the bedroom. I'd learned humanizing the victim too much made it harder for me to do my job. It was already hard because I had such fond memories of Mrs. McGowen. But I couldn't look away from the photographs that covered the walls. Pictures of two young people madly in love at different stages in their lives. There were no modern photographs. It's like time had stopped for Mrs. McGowen when her husband had passed away.

As we entered the hallway, we faced an extra large mirror, and I could see my full reflection. The only part of me not covered was my eyes and the top of my head.

"The room on the left belongs to the cats," Jack said. "Their litter boxes and food and water bowls are in there. There's one of those play things they can climb on and a bunch of toys scattered about. Oddly enough, it's the cleanest room in the house."

I followed Jack toward the room on the right. There was another door adjacent to the master bedroom, and I assumed it was the bathroom. Jack confirmed it.

"That's the bathroom," he said and then opened the door where Mrs. McGowen's body lay.

My feet squelched into the carpet the moment I stepped into the room, and I was determined not to look down. It was better to focus on the body lying in front of us than anything else.

Death was never pretty. There were deaths that were peaceful and those that were violent in nature. But the beauty of life was always absent. Death had left Mrs. McGowen unrecognizable.

It made sense to assume at first glance that she'd taken a

fall that had eventually ended her life. It happened all the time to the elderly, especially to those who lived alone. They'd fall or have a stroke or heart attack, and there'd be no one there to call for help. They'd sometimes lay for hours or days before finally succumbing to death. It was always sad to find those cases, and in my own mind, one of the most horrible ways to die. Broken, alone, and forgotten.

I'd also learned through the years to never jump to conclusions.

Jack and I had established a rhythm since we'd been working together in an official capacity. I knew he'd already drawn his own conclusions, just as I knew he'd pick up on things that I wouldn't and vice-versa. He let me enter the room and then got out of the way. This was my time now.

Mrs. McGowen, what was left of her, was crumpled on the floor like a ragdoll against the wall, only a few feet inside the door. A round Queen Anne table leaned haphazardly against a reading chair, and a white ceramic lamp lay broken on the floor next to her. The tattered remains of her dressing gown were soaked with blood—almost black in color.

"Why is her dress moving?" I asked. I already knew the answer, but I was hoping it was just a hallucination.

"Insect activity," Jack said. "Apparently, Mrs. McGowen wasn't running her AC yet. The last couple of days have been pretty warm."

"There's going to be no tissue samples left for me after the cats and maggots. I won't be able to do anything other than take measurements and x-rays."

I moved farther into the bedroom. It wasn't an overly large room, but there was space for the queen size bed. It had a white ironwork headboard and footboard with ornate finials at each post. A wedding ring quilt in different shades of purple covered the bed, and there was a lamp on the nightstand to the left of the bed, along with a notebook, pen and a rotary phone. But the nightstand on the right was empty.

The nightstands each sat in front of a window with lace curtains that did nothing for privacy, but gave a beautiful view of the backyard garden. Purple lilac bushes surrounded the perimeter of the backyard, which was why I assumed she felt comfortable with lace curtains since the bushes were as dense and tall as any fence could be.

I took initial photographs, getting several of the positioning of the body, and then moved in closer. The carpet was saturated with blood, so I dug in my bag for the clear plastic tarp and laid it next to her so I could kneel down.

"The cats did a number on her," I said. "If she does have any external wounds, they'll be difficult to find unless damage was done to the bone."

I took more pictures, starting at the head, and then let the camera drop against my chest. "The cats wouldn't have let her body go cold before they started scavenging," I said. "They'd start with soft tissues areas first. Eyes and lips and earlobes."

I gently turned her head so Jack could see. All that was left of her face was the skeletal remains. Her silver hair lay on the floor like a small animal. "The maggots would have done the soft tissue work between the face and the skull, burrowing in and releasing the skin and hair follicles.

That's why her hair is on the floor. And seven cats would make short work of her."

I moved down the torso with the camera, and then zoomed in where the stomach should have been. I'd never been squeamish about the human body. Death was a reality, and there were limitless ways for the body to die. I didn't get the opportunity to see much of those variations working for King George County, but when I had been working hundred hour weeks as an ER doc at Augusta General, I'd seen all kinds of things. But I really hated maggots.

The truth was, very little of my work dealt with homicides, but that's what excited the press, so when I did have one I always got news coverage. Most of the bodies that came across my table were regular people who lived everyday lives and then died a normal death. Sometimes, there was no explainable reason for a healthy thirty-year old man to die. And sometimes there wasn't much left to work with at all, just like with Mrs. McGowen. But those were the cases that interested me most.

I tried to ignore the constant moving beneath the remains of Mrs. McGowen's housecoat, but I couldn't avoid it forever, so I carefully cut open her clothes, the fabric hard with dried blood.

"There are two stages of insect activity," I told Jack. "The eggs would've been laid and hatched within the first twenty-four hours of her death. But it could've been sooner with the heat, accelerating the process. A few of these maggots are mature adults, but most have just been hatched, which means she's been dead long enough for a second generation. In normal temperatures, you're looking at six to ten days. But with the heat, maybe three to five."

And it was hot in the house. The AC wasn't on, the windows were shut tight, and though I'd seen ceiling fans in a couple of the rooms and there was a box fan in the corner, they weren't on and there wasn't even a hint of a breeze.

"We still have to canvas the neighborhood and see if anyone saw her after her banana bread delivery, but that timeline works if she died sometime late Sunday or early Monday morning," Jack said. "The bed is made and she's in her night clothes, so she either hadn't gone to bed yet, or she was already up for the day.

"It's easy enough to lose balance and take a header at her age. I'll check her for broken bones once I get back to the lab and can do x-rays. If she broke a hip or a leg, she wouldn't have been able to get back up. The pain could've sent her into cardiac arrest, though her heart is missing so it's just conjecture.

"Let's say you're right and she tripped and fell. We have to assume she was incapacitated to the point that she couldn't even make an attempt to reach the phone. Look at the way her body fell. The way she's facing, as if she were entering the room. If she'd tripped, she would have fallen forward, right? Maybe breaking her fall with her hands. But she fell backward and to the side, away from us."

"So maybe a stroke or heart attack," I said, seeing it clearly. "She just dropped where she was. Her left side would be pretty banged up from hitting the table, and she'd probably have hit her head against the wall or floor."

"I want you to look for things that might not result in a death from natural causes."

I raised my brows. "You think she could've been murdered?"

That had not been what I was expecting. But Jack was a hell of a cop, and if he was asking, it was because he had a reason. Sometimes the reason was only his gut, but it was enough for me.

# 3

"I CAN'T DO ANYTHING ELSE HERE," I SAID. "I SHOULD have an answer for you in a couple of hours though. I'm going to bring in the team and get her out of here."

I got to my feet and stretched out my back, feeling a couple of vertebrae crack. "Just out of curiosity, why am I looking for a COD other than natural causes?"

"Did you notice the windows?" Jack asked.

I waited for my brain to shift gears and think about the investigation outside the body, but I was coming up at a loss with the windows. They looked like regular windows to me. "What about them?" I asked.

"This one here and one in the living room." He moved to the window to the right of the bed. "The curtains got shut in the window when it was closed. If you look past the damage done by the cats, I think you'll find that Mrs. McGowen was very neat and tidy." He opened the closet door and inside were perfectly folded sweaters on a shelf, clothes hung by color, and shoes in labeled shoe boxes.

"Everything has a place. I've never seen closets as organized as these before."

"So someone else wasn't quite as careful," I said.

"The kitchen is the same," he said. "It's the only room in the house she's modernized. It's state of the art. Pans, dishes, cookbooks. Everything is in meticulous order. Except there's dishes in the sink and an empty pan on the floor."

"From the banana bread for the neighbors?"

"Hard to tell. Common sense tells me there'd be a lot more dishes or…something. This seems more simple. Two mixing bowls in the sink and an empty pan."

"You'd have a much better guess in that area that I would," I said.

"Very true. Suzy Homemaker you will never be."

I could see the grin in his eyes, though his mouth was covered by the mask.

"My talents lie in other areas."

"So I've discovered. Have I told you I'm grateful?" he asked.

"Not since eleven-fifty-three last night when you slapped me on the butt and told me good game."

"I was showing good sportsmanship. How come I didn't get a slap on the butt?"

"Because I was comatose and face-down on the mattress. You know it was a good game when that happens. And stop fishing for compliments. We were talking about *my* talents."

The front door opened and the sound of muted voices could be heard as my assistant and one of the interns made their way with the gurney to the bedroom.

Sheldon Durkus needed a job so he could work his way through mortuary school, and I'd needed an assistant. It had seemed like the stars had aligned when he'd answered my ad for employment. In the month since I'd hired him, he'd caught on quickly as long as what he was working on was in the lab. It was living people he wasn't so great with. I'd questioned more than once whether being a mortician was in his future, as it was necessary to be sympathetic to the living while taking care of their loved ones. The sympathy gene seemed to have passed right through Sheldon.

Sheldon was what I liked to call pocket-sized. He was a few inches shorter than I was, and though he wasn't overweight, he was doughy. He had a full head of black curly hair and a pencil-thin mustache that was so fine it looked like dirt smudges. He was a cross between Rob Schneider and a Cabbage Patch Kid. He was dressed in an army green coveralls that he'd been given at mortuary school, and he wore a supply pack on his back—like a Ghostbuster.

"Doctor Graves," he said as he entered the room, pulling the gurney behind him. And then he stopped as he caught sight of the victim.

"Why are her clothes moving?" he asked.

"Maggots."

I won't lie. I found a little satisfaction in the fact that he turned an unusual shade of green, and I was glad I was wearing the surgical mask so my smile didn't show. I snuck a look at Jack and could see the laugh lines at the corners of his eyes.

"Ohmigod," another voice said from the doorway.

Lily Bennet was my new intern. She had the face of a supermodel, the body of a Kardashian, and the brain of a scholar. She was close to six feet tall and her mink colored hair was pulled up in a high ponytail and waved halfway down her back. Every police officer in the county had tried making a move on her. No one had succeeded.

Statistically, it was ridiculous that she had just about everything possible going for her. Plus, she was just sarcastic enough that it was hard to hate her. I actually really liked her. She was still inexperienced, but she'd eventually make a hell of a dead doctor. Why she'd chosen to go the forensic pathologist route instead of being a surgeon where she could make the big bucks was beyond me, but she seemed determined, and I was getting someone with an exceptional skill set and brain for free.

"Well," she said. "That's unexpected."

"A group of cats is called a clowder," Sheldon said. "So technically, the victim was eaten by a clowder of cats. In case it needs to go in the report."

There was an awkward pause while we all stared at Sheldon, and he wiped at the sweat on his upper lip.

"Right," I said, thinking it probably *would* have to go in the report. "We're going to have to be careful in transport. The meat between the remaining skin and bone is gone, so it'll shift if we're not careful. Bring everything with her in the bag."

"How do we move her without dislodging the skin?" Lily asked.

The skin had dried out without the moisture of blood beneath it and looked somewhat mummified.

"The best way I've found is with straps or towels," I said. "Our hands can do a lot of damage to sensitive tissues. Put a towel beneath each limb and use it to lift her into the bag. Let's get her wrapped up. I've reached my tolerance level for smells for the day."

I supervised to make sure they got the body into the bag okay, and then left them to finish up with the gurney. I followed Jack back out to the front porch. The air, warm as it was, was refreshing and I took off my mask, sucking in a deep breath. Jack did the same.

"I need to get a clear picture of her day to day routine," he said. "I'm going to have the boys catalog this like a crime scene. I'd rather be safe than sorry. Who knows, maybe my gut is still on vacation."

We'd only been back from our honeymoon for a couple of weeks, and things had been very slow leading into summer. It made it nice because we'd fallen into a routine of sorts, each getting home from work at reasonable hours and usually having time to eat lunch together during the day.

"Something just feels off here," he said. "The people on this street know everything about each other, what they're doing and when they're doing it. She's been dead for three days. Someone had to have seen something."

"That might be the point," I said. "If no one saw anything in a neighborhood like this, maybe she did slip and fall."

"That would certainly be the preferable explanation. I just want to make sure. I've already called in for a search warrant. It's easy enough to justify for a search of what could've contributed to her death, especially since the cats destroyed the body."

Jack checked his watch as Sheldon and Lily rolled the gurney out the front door, and we all lifted it down the stairs. It had never happened to me, but I'd witnessed an EMT lose his grip on a gurney before and drop a victim. It wasn't pretty. And it was never good in front of an audience.

"Let's meet back here when you're finished and we'll do some door to doors. I'm anxious to talk to the neighbors."

I was too, but I wasn't sure if it was because I was nosy or because Jack had stirred something in me that was making me look at the scene from a different angle. The best thing I could do was get back to the lab and get started.

---

GRAVES FUNERAL HOME was on the corner of Catherine of Aragon and Anne Boleyn. As far as locations went, it was a good one. It was close enough to the cemetery that it was convenient for the families of the deceased, and close enough to the Town Square that my signage was a good advertisement to passersby.

There was a strip mall across the street that held a myriad of revolving businesses, but over the past month or so, the owners had given it a facelift and repaved the parking lot. The laundromat was still there, but a delicatessen had just opened in the corner unit, and a Crate and Go had opened in one of the middle units. There was a sign advertising that a Crossfit gym was coming soon, and I wondered if the convenience of it would give me the incentive to work out. I figured the answer to that was no unless they were giving away free hot fudge sundaes after every workout session.

I'd hitched a ride in the Suburban to come back to the funeral home, and we turned onto Catherine of Aragon. The Suburban was black and had large magnetic stickers on each side, advertising the funeral home, so it wasn't like we were covert. Much of the traffic had pulled to the side with curious drivers watching us pass by. By this time of the morning, word around town would have spread about Mrs. McGowen's death, and most everyone would know we were transporting her body.

The funeral home was Colonial in style—three full stories of red brick with white columns. Two elm trees were planted in front, one on each side of the sidewalk, and they shaded the entire yard. There was a portico attached to the side where we parked the Suburban, and a ramp to the side door that led into a special foyer, the kitchen, and the door of my lab.

It had been my parents who'd put in the state of the art lab in the basement. It had a solid steel door that could only be opened with a numerical passcode. I hadn't understood the need for such secrecy until I'd discovered what they were doing with the bodies down there. But now that I was coroner for the county, I was glad to have top of the line equipment and plenty of space to work in. Many small county coroners didn't have that luxury.

I uncoded the door and felt the change in temperature as the door opened. The lights came on automatically and we pushed the gurney onto the lift to the left of the stairs. The lift was big enough for two people and a gurney, so I took the metal stairs and met them at the bottom.

The room was utilitarian and cold in design. The floor was industrial white tile with a couple of drains built in just in case it needed to be hosed down. The shelves against the wall were steel and filled with various tools and microscopes. I had one stainless steel autopsy table and one embalming table. They were built with what I called a moat around the edges so bodily fluids could drain properly. On the autopsy table, the drain led to a biohazard sink with a drain-catch at the bottom, just in case something important got washed down. There were high powered spray hoses mounted on the wall behind each table, and at the opposite end of the autopsy table was a scale so I could weigh the organs. Which was not going to be an issue at all with Mrs. McGowen.

On the wall adjacent to the tables was a curing cabinet where I hung blood soaked evidence to dry. To the right side of my tables was the walk-in refrigeration unit that could store up to six bodies.

We rolled Mrs. McGowen over to the autopsy table.

"On three," I said. "One, two, three…" And we lifted the black bag onto the table. We got her unzipped and used the towels again to remove the bag from beneath her. Many of the maggots remained in the bag.

"Go ahead and put those in one of the sample jars," I told Lily.

I'd stripped out of my outer coveralls before we'd left Mrs. McGowen's, and it was shoved into a plastic so I could wash it later. I put my hair in a net and donned a plastic apron, tying it behind my waist. Then I put on a fresh pair of gloves.

"Doctor Graves." Emmy Lu's voice came through the intercom. "The cats are in the mudroom. They're loud. Tyler is in there with them gathering samples. I think he's going to need a tetanus shot. What do you want to do with them after he's done?"

Tyler was my other intern, and he was pretty much Lily's opposite in every way in the looks department. He was a bright kid, but weird. Not Sheldon weird, but another kind of weird altogether. He needed a lot of life experience. And probably a girlfriend and less weed. He was the perfect person to deal with the cats.

"Just give Doc Mooney a call over at the vet and see if he can send someone to get them cleaned up and checked out. Maybe put out some feelers to see if they can be found homes. A diet of human can't be good for their digestive system."

"Will do," Emmy Lu said. "Also, Marilyn Richardson is here for your eleven o'clock appointment about her husband."

"Damn," I muttered under my breath.

"Quarter," Lily and Sheldon said at the same time.

I'd forgotten I had appointments lined up for the day. That

was one of the reasons I'd hired Emmy Lu though. She kept things on track when I couldn't.

"I'm going to send up Sheldon," I said. And then I thought about it for a second and broke out in a cold sweat. I needed to keep business and make sure the customers were happy. "And Lily too," I added.

Lily must have read the panic in my eyes at the thought of Sheldon meeting with Mrs. Richardson by himself, and she nodded in agreement and took off her coveralls and gloves.

"Mrs. Richardson's husband is on hospice," I reminded them. "He's expected to pass in the next couple of days, so be sympathetic to that. A lot of times it's hard for them to make decisions ahead of time. She might second guess herself. A lot of times they've convinced themselves that there's still hope for recovery. She's got a mid-range budget, so steer her toward the steel caskets with the satin lining."

"Did you know that in the Iron Age, throwing spears at corpses was the equivalent of a twenty-one-gun salute?" Sheldon asked. "It was quite an honor."

"I don't think that's in Mrs. Richardson's budget," I said, deadpan.

Lily snorted and covered it with a cough, and then followed Sheldon back upstairs to where Mrs. Richardson would be waiting.

I waited until the door closed behind them and then grabbed the remote, turning on my Spotify playlist. I was feeling mellow and chose Billy Joel's "She's Always A Woman to Me". Once I got into my work, I barely noticed that the music was there, but it was nice having a little background noise to keep me company.

I grabbed a clipboard and pen. The first thing I had to do was give an accurate description of the body as I'd received it and catalog everything. Height, weight, what she was wearing, and then any jewelry or distinguishing marks—like tattoos or birthmarks.

The only thing she'd been wearing was a nightgown that snapped down the front and came to mid-calf. It had been blue with tiny white flowers on it. I'd had to look hard to find an area that actually had blue left. I carefully unbuttoned the gown and cut the sleeves so I didn't have to move her body too much. Then I took the remnants and hung it in the curing cabinet so the wet blood could dry.

There were no organs left and the remaining maggots clung to the soft tissue, so a true autopsy was impossible, but I went over the body inch by inch with my UV light and magnifier, checking the skin for marks or bruising that was difficult to see with the naked eye. I paused when I reached her left hand and saw the simple gold wedding band, much too big for the bony finger it clung to. I removed it carefully and put it in a plastic baggie. She had no other jewelry and her skin was too damaged for me to see much of anything else.

Before I could really delve into the body, I had to get rid of the remaining maggots. Unfortunately, there was really no easy way to do so except to remove them one by one. I grabbed a jar and forceps and got to work.

By the time I was done, the last chords of Elton John's "Goodbye Yellow Brick Road" were fading and I was holding a jar full of squirming maggots. I put them to the side and then readied the x-ray machine. Once I had the x-rays in hand, I took them to the light board and snapped in the images.

"I'll be damned," I said, and then looked around just to make sure no one had heard me. "Jack was right."

# 4

I FINISHED UP AND LEFT LILY AND SHELDON TO BOIL MRS. McGowen down to the bones. I tried to call Jack but it went straight to voice mail.

The funeral home was fully functional on all floors, but we generally kept the third floor off-limits since it was rare to have multiple viewings on the same night. But the space closest to my lab was for employees only.

There was a kitchen next to the lab door, and behind the kitchen was an office with a full bathroom attached. I kept several changes of clothes for all occasions in the closet. I was never quite sure what I smelled like when I came out of the lab, so I usually played it safe and took a quick shower before I had to move amongst the general public.

I dressed in black ankle length slacks, black ballet flats, and a black blouson top with three-quarter sleeves. I wore black out of habit as I'd found it was the most forgiving color when faced with the mess of death. I didn't expect to come into contact with another body today, but one could never be too sure. Stranger things had happened.

I grabbed a fresh cup of coffee and a granola bar from the kitchen and headed back to Mrs. McGowen's house. Jack's unit was the only vehicle left at the scene when I arrived. The neighbors had gone back to their lives and jobs and the street was empty. At least from the outside. I saw the curtains move from the house to the right when I pulled into the driveway.

Jack was coming around from the back of the house by the time I got out of the Suburban. He'd changed clothes since I'd last left him, and I knew he must've been cat-deep in the bowels of that house as they'd gone through everything. He wore a plain black T-shirt and jeans, and he looked worn out. He'd removed his duty belt while he'd been working, but he still carried his revolver in his ankle holster.

"You made good time," he said. "I thought you'd be at least another hour."

"There wasn't much I could do with her. I've got her boiling in the pot for now so I can check the bones later."

Jack's smile turned to somewhat of a grimace at the mention of the boiling pot. "I take it that means you found something worth checking?"

I grinned, excitement making the hairs on my scalp tingle. "I tried calling, but it went to voice mail. You were right," I told him and held up the first x-ray. "She's got a fracture on the parietal. Look at the impact. That's blunt force trauma. Nothing she fell against would have done that kind of damage. She was hit with something with a sharp edge. And something with weight to it by the depth of the indention. I'll do a mold of the wound once she's out of the boiler."

"We didn't find anything around the body that would fit that description," he said. "I'll call in and have Nash and Cheek start doing a search in a three-block radius. Maybe they'll find a murder weapon that matches."

I waited while he made the call and then showed him the next x-ray once he hung up. "Look at the right ulna," I said. "It's fractured. Defensive wound." And then I demonstrated by putting my right arm in front of my face for protection. "The first strike broke her arm. The second struck her in the parietal, left side of the skull."

"So the assailant was right handed," Jack said, "along with most of the population."

"Hey, you have your homicide. Now we just need motive, a murder weapon, and a suspect."

"Is that all?" Jack asked wryly. He reached out and touched the bottom of my hair, tugging it just a little before he let go.

I wanted to lean into him, but I knew there were eyes everywhere. "You finished here?" I put the x-rays back in the car and locked the door.

"Yes, though I'd stay clear of Nash if I were you. He's got a whole lot of cat poop to deliver to your doorstep."

"Then it was well worth the twenty," I said, grinning.

"I'm going to have the team come back and dust for prints around the windows. Maybe we'll get lucky. There was no sign of forced entry, and it's impossible to know if anything was taken at this point. She had a pill dispenser in the bathroom. There was no cell phone, but we found a charger for one in her car."

"Do you think she let in the killer?"

"Hard to say, but I think someone would've noticed on this street if she'd had company over. We'll find out when we do the door-to-doors. But there was a slight disturbance in the flowerbed beneath her bedroom window. One of the plants looked like it had been partially stepped on, but we didn't find any shoe prints."

At that moment, Officer Chen and Detective Martinez pulled into the driveway next to Jack in a marked unit. They'd both changed into street clothes since I'd seen them that morning. Chen wore black slacks and a black sleeveless top, her badge worn on a lanyard around her neck so it was visible. Martinez wore jeans and a tan button-down with the King George Sheriff's Office logo above the breast pocket. His badge was clipped to his belt. Both of their weapons were visible.

"Hey, Sheriff," Martinez said as they got out of the car. "We unloaded the last of the evidence boxes in the conference room. Then we spent a little time in the decontamination chamber. Just so you know, I'm gonna need a raise after today. This was some sick shit."

Jack grinned. "But all worth it to see Nash go ass over elbows in kitty litter."

"Chen got pictures of it," Martinez said. "It's the most

beautiful artwork I've ever seen. She even blew them up real big so you can see them clearly."

"I thought the bullpen needed a little decoration," Chen said straight-faced. "I'd like to request traffic duty tomorrow, to put a little distance between myself and Nash."

"She means he's going to be pissed," Martinez said. "I can't wait to see it."

"We're all going to be neck deep in cat guts tomorrow, but maybe we can get Betsy to record it for us." He caught what he was saying and then amended it to, "Or someone else."

Betsy Clement had been the secretary for the sheriff's office for forty years. I was doubtful she'd be able to record anything. She still used an electric typewriter and did payroll by hand because she was afraid of the computer that had been sitting on her desk for two years and never been turned on.

"I hope you're kidding about cat guts," Martinez said. "I'd hate to have to resign. Nothing I saw in the army compared to what those cats did to that lady."

"The cats are done. The murder investigation isn't."

"Murder investigation?" Chen asked, eyes narrowed.

"Someone bashed Rosalyn McGowen over the head with a heavy object. I've got Nash and Cheek canvassing the area to see if the murder weapon was dumped."

"It was something with a sharp corner," I added. "I'll make a mold once her bones are ready."

"We think TOD was sometime between Sunday night and

Monday morning. We need a timeline. You guys take the houses across the street and start doing door to doors. This is the kind of neighborhood where everyone knows everything. I want to know it all. Get the dirt and let's see if we can put a solid board together. Jaye and I will do this side and the cul-de-sac. You can head home after, but send me the report once you've got it written up. We'll meet in the morning at nine in the conference room. There's something unusual about this case. Once word gets out she was murdered we're going to be under close scrutiny. Everything stays close to the vest."

"People are going to start to panic," Martinez said. "Another one of our own murdered. It's the most we've had in the last several years."

"We'll find whoever did this. There are bad people in the world. That's just the truth of it. They want to cause harm. All we can do is try to stop them before they start or hunt them after. This time we're hunting."

Chen and Martinez headed across the street to the house at the end of the block, and I turned to Jack.

"Are people really going to panic?"

"Some might. Citizens don't like it when their crime rate goes up. And the only person to blame is me. We'll find out how much they blame me come election time."

"That's ridiculous," I said defensively. "You're the best sheriff this county has ever had. The world is just changing. It's more dangerous everywhere. And people are nuts."

Jack smiled, but it was distant. "Let's talk to the neighbors and see what they have to say."

“It’s after noon,” I said. “Do you think anyone is going to be home?”

Jack snorted out a laugh. “All the curtains on this street have been flapping back and forth so much I can feel the draft. I don’t think anyone went to work today.”

“Just an FYI…I left Sheldon and Lily to deal with my appointments today, so we might have to sell the funeral home to pay our bills. And we’ll probably have to move to Canada.”

“Why Canada? That seems drastic,” Jack said. “And we can pay our bills for twenty lifetimes even if you have to sell the funeral home. We’re rich. Problem solved. Stop worrying.”

“Did you know they used to throw spears at a corpse in the Iron Age? Like a twenty-one-gun salute. It was a great honor.”

“Is this a new service you’re providing?”

“Sheldon’s going to include it on our option sheet,” I said, pretty much resigned to whatever outcome he led us to.

“I’m sure Lily will have things well under control. And if not, she’s a black belt so maybe she’ll knock him unconscious.”

We walked to the house to the right of Mrs. McGowen’s and a young woman in her mid-twenties answered the door before we’d walked onto her porch. She was a pretty girl, blonde and blue-eyed, with her hair piled on top of her head in a messy bun. She was heavily pregnant and had a little girl on her hip who couldn’t have been more than two. She looked familiar, but I couldn’t place her.

"Hey, Katie," Jack said and then winked at the little girl. "Do you have a few minutes?"

"Sure, y'all come on in," she said. "I just made a pitcher of tea if you'd like some."

"Sounds great," Jack said. "I don't know if you've had the chance to meet Doctor Graves." And then Jack turned to me. "Katie is Stewart's daughter," he explained.

Now I realized why I recognized her. Captain Stewart Smith had been a cop for a lot of years, and his family was practically an institution in Bloody Mary. His mother was Martha Smith, who owned Martha's diner. Half the people in Bloody Mary were related to the Smith's in one way or the other.

"Oh, nice to meet you," I said.

"You too. I saw your wedding announcement in the paper. Congratulations. My dad said it was about time."

Jack laughed and we sat on a little couch next to the front with that looked out over the street. *One Life to Live* was playing on the television, but it was on mute.

"And don't worry about that mean old Madam Scandal," she said. "I didn't believe a word of her story. I'll get your tea and be back in a second."

Her smile was sweet and she put the little girl in a play area that looked like a big cage with a baby gate on it. There were toys inside of it and a bowl of Cheerio's that had partially spilled on the floor. As far as containment went, it seemed to do the job.

"What's she talking about? What story?" Jack asked.

"The one where you're cheating on me with the floozy you were doing it with in the back of your Tahoe. Madam Scandal was watching from afar."

"I hope she didn't see me knee myself in the forehead. That would be embarrassing." He rubbed at the spot and my lips twitched with laughter. "We probably shouldn't do that again."

"Or maybe just move to the backseat where there's more room. I find the older I get, the more comfortable I like to be. Like going to a concert. I want to pay for the expensive seats so I can sit down the whole time and avoid teenagers standing up in front of me."

"How old are you?" Jack asked, cocking his head. "A hundred?"

"Shut up. Remember how we got invited to go camping, but you found out we'd have to sleep in a tent instead of a hotel so you said no?"

"I just didn't want an audience when we made love. You're a screamer. Besides, there are certain luxuries one deserves after a certain age and income level."

Katie came back in the room and set our tea on coasters on the coffee table in front of us, and Jack took out the red notebook he habitually carried and a pen to take notes.

"I can imagine you're here about Mrs. McGowen." She took the soft recliner across from us and tucked her legs beneath her in the chair. "It's just awful. She was the sweetest woman. When Callie was born she knitted her a blanket and brought over all kinds of food so I didn't have to cook."

"Are you home most days with Callie?" Jack asked.

Katie rolled her eyes and rubbed a hand over her taut stomach. "I don't get out much. Jeremy, that's my husband," she said, looking at me. "He's a junior partner over at Crichton and Hutch, which means he does all the work with less pay, so he's gone most of the time. It'll pay off eventually when he makes partner, but right now things are tough.

"I'll get out to the grocery store on Monday mornings. We go to Martin Grocery because Callie likes that Mrs. Martin gives her animal crackers to snack on while we shop. We're usually done by ten o'clock so we can get home for Callie's nap. I like to take one too," she said, smiling mischievously. "I could sleep sixteen hours a day. This baby has drained all my energy." She looked at me conspiratorially and I couldn't help but smile. "I figure it must be a boy. Only a man can leave you that tired."

I snorted out a laugh and took a drink.

"Umm…let's see," she continued. "On Tuesday and Thursday at nine, I take Callie to play group, but that's pretty much it. I spend most of my time on this street, visiting with neighbors or working on various projects. The Millers—they own the big house in the middle of the cul-de-sac—they let me and Callie come down and use the pool."

"Did you see Mrs. McGowen pretty regularly?" Jack asked. "At certain times or on certain days?"

"Oh, sure," Katie said, taking a sip of her tea. "Rosie always said that idle hands were the devil's workshop. She got up about four o'clock every morning and started baking. I could sometimes smell her cinnamon rolls. There was nothing like the smell of those cinnamon rolls. My mouth is watering just thinking about them. And they tasted even better. I could eat a truck full of those rolls."

"When are you due?" I asked.

"Three weeks. It's not going to be too long before we outgrow this house. I've always wanted to be a stay at home mom. Rosie would come over some afternoons and show me a recipe or two, walking me through it. I never had the hand at it like she did, but I can bake better than most. My husband usually goes in late for work when I get up to bake, so it's nice to spend the extra time with him."

"When was the last time you saw her?" Jack asked.

"She brought banana bread on Sunday afternoon. About three o'clock. Carl was with her. She's very independent, and she'd sometimes stack everything on her walker and haul it up and down the street, but Carl stopped her and insisted he carry the basket. She brought me two loaves."

"You didn't see her any time after that?" I asked.

"I didn't *see* her," Katie said. "I heard her. She doesn't like turning on her air conditioner until she has to. She lives on a fixed income, so she was real particular about that stuff. So she'd open all her windows and turn on her fans. She'd sleep with them open like that, but it's not something you really have to worry about in this neighborhood. We do it sometimes too."

"What do you mean you heard her?" Jack asked.

"She was real independent, like I said, still driving herself everywhere and things like that. But her hearing wasn't so good. She'd turn her TV up real loud at night, so it was easy to hear with the windows open. But it didn't really bother me. She always turned it off and went to bed about eight."

"You heard her TV on Sunday night?"

"Yes, but I got busy because Callie had a fever, and Jeremy didn't get home until after nine. I was up on and off through the night, but I saw her lights on and could smell something baking when I got up to check on Callie about five. I crashed pretty soon after that though. Callie's fever broke and I put her in bed with me. I don't think we woke up until close to noon."

"Is there anyone in the neighborhood who didn't get along with Mrs. McGowen?" Jack asked.

Katie paused and thought about the question. "It's hard to say. It's a real friendly street for the most part, but people are people. They get into it over silly things and then they're fine the next day. The Brights live two houses down from Rosie. No one really gets along with them, but they mostly stay to themselves, so I can't say if they had an issue with Rosie. She brought them banana bread anyway.

"There are just little snipes here and there. Janet Selby tried real hard to get Rosie to move to assisted living just so she could sell the house for her and get commission. Janet was rather put out that Rosie said no. And one time, one of Rosie's cats got out and Harrison Taylor found it on the hood of his Porsche. You'd have thought someone had taken a tire iron to it the way he reacted. He called the cops and tried to have the cat put down."

"We went to school with Harrison Taylor," I told her. "It sounds like he hasn't changed much."

Katie snorted in disbelief. "He's a word I can't say in front of a two-year old. He and his wife are a pair. JoAnn likes her margaritas, and she's usually half-lit at any neighborhood function we have. I can't blame her since she's married to Harrison. But she used to drive Rosie crazy, always telling her she needed to publish her recipes and how she could help her get it done. And of course, they could split the profits." Katie rolled her eyes. "JoAnn knows as much about cooking and publishing as she knows about modesty. I think it made Rosie uncomfortable though. She was very protective of her recipes. Rosie used to say a woman didn't get to be her age without learning how to keep a good secret."

"Can you give me a rundown on the rest of the street?" Jack asked.

"Oh, sure," she said. "That's easy. Doug Roland lives next door. He retired from the Army several years ago, but he likes to travel, so he's rarely home. When he is home, he has a lady friend that comes to visit about three times a week. He never comes to any of the neighborhood stuff. In his words, 'I hate that crap.'"

She stopped and tried to find a comfortable position in the chair, but I figured the only way she'd be comfortable again was to give birth.

"The Middletons live right across the street from Doug. They're newlyweds. Monica is a nurse and works days, and Doug works nightshift security somewhere on Capitol Hill. I think he goes to school during the day, so he's rarely home." Katie looked as if she was going to say something else, but she paused.

"What is it?" Jack asked.

"Not my business really. I've just noticed a couple of times Monica has had someone over during the night. I got an ice cream craving one night and went out about midnight. I could see two people moving around in the house, but there was no car in driveway. Someone could easily park on one of the side streets and cut through the woods. No one would see them. I just feel bad, you know? Doug's a nice guy, and he's working really hard."

"Was she friends with Mrs. McGowen?"

"Not really. They were friendly, and Monica usually does participate in the neighborhood events, but she's got her own life that's separate. She seems a very private person.

"Next door to Doug and Monica is Clark and Maria Green. That's the house directly across from this one. Maria is a few months behind me in her pregnancy, so I've been able to give her lots of maternity clothes.

"Jenson and Angela Davis live next door to them, right across from Rosie. They're nice, but quiet. They've got two kids that walk over to the elementary school, and I've seen them next door getting cookies and lemonade with the other kids. Abby Clearwater lives next to them. She just moved in last year, so no one knows her very well. She teaches at the high school. Harrison Taylor took a liking to her right off. Poor girl can't shake him. I told you he's a piece of work. A few months after Callie was born, he made a pass. He grabbed my—" She paused and then spelled A-S-S. "He passed it off as an accident when I told him to keep his hands to himself. I started carrying mace. Abby got one for all the women on the street after he started hassling her."

"None of the men have gotten into it with Taylor for making unwanted advances?" Jack asked.

"There's definitely tension there, but Harrison likes to throw his weight around. He makes veiled threats about having loans recalled or investigating trumped up complaints. He's the DA, so there's not a lot anyone can do."

What she said was the truth. No one had as much power as the DA. The good news was Harrison was up for reelection in November. I hoped he lost. He was a real horse's ass.

"Of course, Carl and Robert live on the other side of Rosie. Poor Carl is the one who found her this morning. They were close. He was more like a son to her than a neighbor. Carl works in construction, so he's usually home every day about four o'clock, but Robert works from home. Robert is Carl's husband.

"I've already told you about the Brights," she said, looking out the window. "They live next door to Carl and Robert. Harrison and JoAnn are next to them on the cul-de-sac. Tom and Lynette Miller live in the big Colonial at the center of the cul-de-sac. They always have the neighborhood parties there because they have a pool. Next door to them is the Selbys. Very Stepford," she said with a shudder.

"They're pretty active in the community. Always coming and going."

Jack closed his notebook. "Katie, if you ever want a job as a cop, let me know. You're very observant."

"My dad would kill me," she said, grinning.

"Did you see Mrs. McGowen any other time this week?" Jack asked. "Did you notice her car gone or her TV too loud?"

"Now that you mention it," she said, "no. It's been a crazy week with Callie being sick, and I've been working on the nursery for the baby. I've been neck deep in paint and ordering the rest of his things online. I have noticed she wasn't gone as much this week. Her car has been right there in the driveway every time I've looked that way."

"Is she gone a lot?" I asked.

"Oh, sure. Rosie was very active, especially down at the senior's center. I personally think she had a boyfriend. She'd sometimes leave late at night and come back before the sun came up the next morning. I'm a light sleeper and our bedroom is right next to her driveway. Jeremy can sleep through anything," she said with exasperation. "Whereas I'm up forty-two times a night to go to the bathroom or trying to find a position so I don't have a foot in my ribs. I figure I can sleep when I'm dead." She winced after she said the words. "That's a horrible thing to say. I'm sorry. I guess we never realize when one breath might be our last. I just hate that she was there by herself at the end. But she never seemed like she was a lonely woman. There was always someone around."

"Did you see any cars in her driveway this week or anyone knocking on her door?" Jack asked.

Katie cocked her head and stared at Jack for a few seconds. "I've got pregnancy brain or I would've caught on faster. I am a cop's daughter, after all. You think someone killed her?" she asked, eyes wide. She glanced over at her daughter as if to make sure no one had snatched her out of her cage.

"We know someone did," I confirmed.

"When? How?" she asked. "I just don't see how that's possible. Nothing happens in this neighborhood. It's the safest place I know. Most people don't even lock their doors."

I wasn't going to say anything, but that seemed like a mistake to me. This wasn't 1983. The news was full of good places where bad things happen because bad people live in the world.

"I didn't see or hear anything unusual," she said. "It's a quiet neighborhood. I haven't noticed any cars out of place. We'll get a lot of walkers and joggers because it's a pretty street, and sometimes cars will pass by to look at the houses. Nothing out of the ordinary."

Jack and I thanked her for the tea and told her not to get up to see us out. She was looking a little peaked. The little girl in the cage was watching *One Life to Live* as if it were oxygen and finishing off her Cheerio's. She didn't even notice we left.

"What do you think?" I asked once we were back outside.

"I think whoever killed Mrs. McGowen knew her routine as well as Katie."

We were back in front of the little gray house. It wouldn't be long before it was all over town that someone had killed her.

"When are your bones going to be done?" he asked.

"Another couple hours or so. I'll have Lily lay them out before she goes home for the day, and I'll take a look at them first thing in the morning."

When I'd first moved back to Bloody Mary after my parents' "deaths", I hadn't been thrilled with the idea of taking over the family business. I was a doctor, and I liked being a doctor. And weirdly enough, I'd liked being an ER doctor, even though the pay wasn't as great as specialists or surgeons and the hours were lousy.

And maybe if the coroner's job hadn't been offered to me I wouldn't have stayed in Bloody Mary, carrying on the family legacy, especially after finding out what my parents had been using the family legacy for. But being a coroner—finding the reasons *why* someone died—made me see a different purpose than just saving lives.

I'd done a rotation in pathology when I was a resident, and I'd enjoyed it. My attending physician had said it was the best kept secret in medicine. You never had to work late and no one was in a hurry because dead people were still dead the next day. It was true, and I found I didn't miss the chaos that working in the ER brought. It was nice to go home to my husband at night and still be awake enough to talk to him.

"Let's go down and talk to Carl," Jack said. "Maybe he can fill in some of the missing pieces."

My nose squenched before I could help it.

"Maybe don't do that when you see him. It was twenty years ago. People change."

"I sure hope so. But just in case, do you think he'd be offended if I shook his hand with my gloves on?"

# 5

I DIDN'T KNOW MUCH ABOUT CARL PLANTER OTHER THAN the rumors that had probably plagued him every moment he spent in Bloody Mary.

The thing about King George County was that it was still south of the Mason Dixon line. People here liked to think that they were progressive thinkers and that things like equality were the norm, but the truth was, we still lived in an area with one of the most active Aryan Nation headquarters, where men were still seen as superior to women, where the LGTBQ community was talked about in hushed tones, and African Americans were watched closely in stores. Change wasn't something easily accepted in the small parts of the country.

Don't get me wrong, there were plenty of great things about King George County. It was a good place to raise a family and patriotism ran strong. But it was a place that preached against judging others, unless the judging happened with a cold beer or a sweet tea. Then it wasn't judging. It was showing neighborly concern while making sure everyone knew someone else's business.

According to Katie, Carl worked in the construction business in some capacity. There was a white Ford-150 parked in the driveway along with a silvery blue Prius. He also lived in my favorite house on the street. I was thinking he'd remodeled it, because it halfway looked like the other houses on the street, but on steroids.

It was a farmhouse-style house with two brick chimneys and a covered front porch with thick raw beams for the posts. The roof was metal, and green baskets of ivy hung evenly spaced between the porch posts. Glass French doors were placed right in the middle of the house and there was a matching pair on the opposite side, so you could see straight through. There weren't coverings on any of the windows. When I looked at the house, I thought of space and light. And that it must be terribly hard to keep the house clean enough for people to be able to look inside all the time.

Jack rang the front doorbell and we only had to wait a few moments for Carl to answer.

"I thought we might get a visit from you two," he said, opening the door wide. "I saw you go down and visit Katie."

"Good to see you again, Carl," Jack said. "It's been a long time."

"Almost twenty years," he said, grinning. "Not near long enough to outrun the rumors that followed me out of town. I guess fantasy was much more exciting than the reality of my mom getting a job offer in Pittsburgh and having to move away."

Jack laughed and acknowledged the elephant in the room. I tried to look like I had no idea what he was talking about.

"I've just poured some iced tea," he said. "Robert is at the kitchen table."

Ahh, iced tea. The South's get-well elixir. I didn't remember Carl all that well from high school. In fact, I probably wouldn't have recognized him if we'd passed on the street. He was well over six-feet and solid in size. He looked like he belonged on a construction site. His jeans were worn and comfortable looking and his blue T-shirt was untucked and frayed around the hem. His feet were bare and he hadn't shaved.

We followed him into a spacious kitchen with a big central island. It had distressed white cabinets, lots of glass, and exposed beams.

"I've got to say I'm in love with your house," I said.

He turned and beamed at me. "Thanks. A lot of love, sweat, and tears went into this place. It was falling down when we bought it a few years ago. It brought the value of the whole neighborhood down. The former owner had neglected it pretty badly. And Robert loves Chip and Joanna Gaines, so it seemed like it was a match made in heaven."

Robert was already sitting at the kitchen table that looked like it had been built from old barn wood. He was a slighter man, maybe five-ten or eleven, and he had a bookish appearance about him. He was also considerably younger than Carl. His blond hair was parted to the left and swooped low over his forehead, and he wore tortoise shell glasses.

He stood when we approached the table, and he wore khakis and a blue button-down shirt. "I'm Robert Planter," he said, holding out a hand.

"Jack Lawson." Jack shook his hand and then said, "This is Doctor Graves. She's the coroner for the county."

"I've read all about you in the paper," Robert said, and then he looked at me with pity and I realized he'd also read all about me in the *King George Tattler*. Apparently the KGT was becoming the news source of choice.

"Y'all have a seat," Carl said, sitting in the chair next to Robert.

"Your garden is beautiful," I said, looking through the bank of windows at the back. It was similar to Rosalyn McGowen's garden, but a little more masculine. An arbor and bridge had been built and was covered with ivy and yellow flowers, and there was a gazebo with a hanging lantern and built-in seating. Flowers were in full bloom, and there was a stack of potting soil bags in a wheelbarrow parked to the side.

"It's my pride and joy," Robert said, his face beaming. "I've ordered a couple of rare rosebushes from England to come in. I've already dedicated the space for them." He pointed to a bed that space had carefully been carved out of. "It's not as easy to order plants from other countries as one might think. They should be in at any time, and then the garden will be perfect."

"Until you see something else on Pinterest you want me to build," Carl said good-naturedly.

"We decided to move back to Bloody Mary about five years ago, but I keep pretty busy with projects, and Robert isn't from here originally so he's still integrating himself in the community. You know how it is. If your family hasn't lived here two hundred years then it's hard to be accepted."

"Yes, I'm sure that's what it is and not the fact that we're probably the only married gay couple in Bloody Mary," Robert said dryly and patted Carl on the hand. "Your naiveté is very attractive, my love."

He said it with such good humor that I couldn't help but smile. He smiled back at me and said, "I work from home, so when we first moved here I wanted to join the quilting club over at The Closet Quilter so I didn't lose my mind staring at walls and a computer screen all day. Plus, the construction going on here was insane. I mean, I figured it was a sign from God with a name like The Closet Quilter. But the blue hairs there were very adamant about me keeping my quilting squares in the closet, if you get my drift. I found a book and wine club I like much better. I haven't read a book yet, but the wine and company is fantastic."

"That must be Crystal Coates' group," I said, leaning my elbows in the table. "I saw her in the grocery store one day and she said they got kicked out of the library because someone had passed out behind the stacks."

"Well, that and the fact that we weren't supposed to have wine in the library."

We all laughed and I asked, "What do you do?"

"I do medical coding for insurance companies, but I do some freelance writing on the side. I've written for several magazines."

"He's working on a book," Carl said proudly. "It's going to be amazing. A bestseller to be sure."

Robert's cheeks pinked in embarrassment, but I could tell he was encouraged by the praise. They were a good couple and fun to talk to.

Carl sighed. "I guess we know why you're here. I stayed home from work today, and we've been trying to have a normal day, pretending I didn't walk in that house and see that this morning. But I'm not going to lie—I think I'll be seeing it every time I close my eyes."

"I read your statement from Officer Chen, but can you walk us through it?" Jack asked. "What made you check on her?"

"I'm a commercial project manager for different construction companies, and I started a big project this week. A new high-rise condo in Richmond. I usually leave around five in the morning, but I've been working a lot of hours this week and decided to go in a couple of hours late. I normally wouldn't have seen her mail because it's so dark when I leave, but I noticed the mailbox was partially opened and stuffed full. That's not like her at all.

"When I get home at four o'clock, she's almost always out getting her mail for the day. She likes to look at the magazines," he said, smiling wistfully. "I've never seen it like that, so I gathered it up and took it to the door. I'd been so busy this week I realized I hadn't seen her and thought she might have gotten sick or something."

"Rosie is always taking care of us," Robert cut in. "She's like a mother for the whole neighborhood. If you're sick, she's going to bring you something to make you better."

"I felt terrible," Carl said, "because Robert's right. She was always the first to come knocking when someone was sick, and we should've been there to do the same for her. I used my key to open the door. She gave me one in case of emergencies. And she's gone away for a couple of days at a time and asked us to feed the cats. I'm allergic to them, so Robert takes care of that chore when she's away. I do the outside stuff, like making sure the lawn is mowed and her garden is watered.

"I could smell something was off when I rang the doorbell. I thought maybe a raccoon or one of the cats had died under the house. Then when I opened the door and saw…" He shook his head and closed his eyes and Robert squeezed his hand.

"Take your time," Robert said, and pushed the tea glass toward him. Carl took it and drank deeply.

"You know how when you see something, but your brain can't process what you're seeing?"

"I do," Jack said, nodding.

"That's exactly what happened. I probably stood there a good five minutes before things started making sense. The smell almost knocked me over, and there was blood everywhere. The cats were running around, obviously distressed.

They looked like they'd gotten into the catnip, they were practically bouncing off the walls.

"I don't know why I called out to her," he said. "But I did. I knew she wouldn't have let the house get like that unless she wasn't able. I just pulled the door closed, got out my phone, and called 9-1-1. They arrived just a few minutes later."

"Katie said you helped Mrs. McGowen deliver banana bread on Sunday," I said.

"I did. She was always trying to do things herself. Never would ask for help. I was sitting out on the porch when I saw her stacking a box on her walker. She never used the walker unless she had to carry something heavy. She got around very well for someone her age. We started at Katie's house and went down to the end of the street. Then across and back up and around the cul-de-sac. We didn't stay and visit anywhere."

"You walked her back to the door when you were finished?"

"I did. It was still daylight outside. Maybe six o'clock or a little after. She liked to be in bed early, but she said she had some work to do."

"Work?" I asked. "More baking?"

"No, no," Carl said. "She was always working on recipes. She had a little laptop. Carried that thing everywhere she went. She said her whole life was on that laptop, and she didn't want anyone getting a hold of it."

"Laptop?" Jack asked. "How big?"

"It was a nice one," he said. "Standard size. She probably spent a couple grand on that thing. She had a case cover on it with a bunch of cupcakes."

Robert jumped in and said, "She said she'd protected her recipes for half a century, and that bigger corporations had been trying to get a hold of them for years, especially when her shop became so profitable and she started doing online orders. She said the big corporations wanted to copyright the recipes and make their own cookbooks, and then she wouldn't be able to sell them anymore. And they weren't above stealing them to get what they wanted."

"Katie said Mrs. McGowen was an early riser," Jack said. "Do you remember noticing if she was up Monday morning when you left for work?"

"Oh, sure," Carl said. "We both noticed because we could smell her cinnamon rolls as we left the house."

"I'm part of the neighborhood running club," Robert said. "We meet Monday, Wednesday and Friday across the street at that house with the For Sale sign in it," he said, pointing out the front window. "We get there a little early to warm up, but soles hit the pavement at five-thirty sharp.

"Those cinnamon rolls are like torture. Rosie doesn't like to run her AC unless it's too hot to stand it, so she'll open the windows and turn on her fans. You can smell cinnamon rolls all over the neighborhood. It's one of the reasons we run," he said, grinning. "Sometimes we'll come back from our three miles and she'll have them waiting for us out on the porch."

"What time did you get back from your run?" Jack asked.

"I was back a little before seven, but everyone's time varies depending on what speed they run or walk. Usually by the mile mark everyone has kind of separated into their groups. I did notice she'd closed the windows by the time I got home because I was looking to see if she was waiting on the porch for us. I won't lie. I was pretty disappointed she wasn't there. I really needed a cinnamon roll."

"Who else is in the running club?" Jack asked.

"Umm…let's see," he said, and then paused in thought. "Me, of course. And Janet Selby. She's in the house kind of cattycorner from us. She usually runs about the same pace I do." He was holding up fingers every time he named someone. "Abby Clearwater is also in our group. She's directly across the street. Harrison Taylor. He's two down from us, but he's one of those who takes off on his own." Robert rolled his eyes. "Harrison thinks a lot of himself. It's not like he's going to the Olympics, but you wouldn't be able to tell by talking to him. He's always finished long before the rest of us get back. Then there's Jenson Davis. He lives next door to Abby. Quiet guy, but he's nice.

"I blew a tire a couple of months ago, and he stopped and helped me change it. He and Monica Middleton are usually the stragglers. He likes a slower pace and she usually has to cut out a little early so she can make it to the hospital on time, so it works for them. And I think Jenson started hanging back with her because Harrison was making her uncomfortable. It's the same reason Abby sticks close to our group. She's much faster than the rest of us, but doesn't want to get alone with Harrison."

"You didn't see Mrs. McGowen any other time this week?" Jack asked both of them.

They shook their heads and Carl said, "It just sickens me to think that she could have been laying there for hours or days, needing help…"

"You'll torture yourself if you keep thinking like that," Robert said.

"He's right," Jack assured him. "There's nothing anyone could've done. Mrs. McGowen was murdered."

# 6

After we left Carl and Robert's house, we moved next door to Frank and Edna Bright. According to Katie, they were retired, spent most of their time at home, and weren't the most pleasant of people. I'd never heard of the Brights and neither had Jack, which meant they were transplants from somewhere.

But Katie had been right—Frank and Edna were two of the most unpleasant people I'd ever met. They were both a few couple of inches over five feet and comfortably plump. They both had white tufts of hair, mean eyes, and they were dressed similarly in Bermuda shorts and socks with their sandals. I'd always heard that people who'd been married a long time started looking like each other, but this was the most obvious example I'd ever witnessed.

"I don't mean to speak ill of the dead," Frank said. He and Edna were sitting on their porch swing, moving it back and forth lazily. Edna was using a paper fan, waving it in front of her face. "But Rosalyn lived the kind of lifestyle where you could expect something like this to happen. An old lady doesn't get murdered for no reason. She wasn't wealthy, living in some mansion with expensive things. She didn't even drive a fancy car. Nah, you mark my words. Rosalyn McGowen wasn't what she seemed." Gleeful spite shone in his eyes.

They hadn't invited us into their cottage-style home. Instead, Jack and I stood on the front porch in the heat.

"What kind of lifestyle is that?" Jack asked.

"A life of secrets," Frank said. "Something seedy. Could've been drugs."

"I think she was a madam," Edna chimed in. "You'd think that laptop was sewn to her skin the way she always carried it around. I think it was a list of her girls she was pimping out. I went down to borrow some brown sugar one afternoon and she had her windows open. Well, I could see right in, couldn't I? She was sitting at her little desk, typing away at that computer. When I rang the doorbell, you would've thought she'd gotten caught with her pants down. Slammed the lid shut and didn't even invite me in when she got the sugar. And the way she was coming and going at all hours of the day and night. Pfft…" Edna flicked her hand like we were supposed to fill in the blanks.

But that statement piqued my interest because Katie had mentioned that Mrs. McGowen sometimes left the house in the middle of the night. She'd thought she'd been meeting a man.

"You'd see her leave at night?" Jack asked.

"Sure. Edna and I are members of the Astronomical Society. When there's a clear night, we'll head over to the area by Gryphon Falls and stargaze. Had a meteor shower last week. There's a great view from the falls. We were just getting in the car when we saw Rosalyn pull out of her driveway. Didn't even have her lights on. She took a right at the stop sign. I tried to see where she was going, but she vanished."

"Did you notice anyone hanging around her home early Monday morning? Maybe a strange car in the area?"

"Hell, no," he scoffed. "We don't keep the same hours as the rest of the nutcases on this street. Everybody up before the crack of dawn like they've got to prove something. People running and saying hi to each other like they didn't just say it the day before. Neighborhood barbecues and picnics. Kids riding their bikes all over the damned street. Harrison Taylor next door tries to rule us all like he's President of the United States instead of president of the neighborhood crime watch. He creeps the hell out of me, but he knows not to come around here. I've got a permit to carry. But I'm telling you, someone killed Roz McGowen for a reason. Everyone on this street has secrets."

"What kind of secrets?" Jack asked.

Frank's grin was oil slick. "Not my place to gossip, but pay attention. You seem like an observant fellow."

---

"We need to find that laptop," Jack said as we made our way next door to the Taylors'. "We searched every inch of that house. There was no laptop. I want to do another walk-through when we're finished. If she was that secretive about her recipes, maybe she had a hidey-hole."

The three houses on the cul-de-sac at the end of Foxglove Court were new additions to the street. They were more than double the size of the other houses and traditionally Georgian in style. The Taylors' was a white two-story with black shutters and an immaculate yard.

Everyone seemed to agree that Harrison Taylor was a prick. I didn't remember him from school, but we hadn't exactly been in the same social circle, which wasn't surprising since he was a few years older.

He'd married JoAnn Godfrey—head cheerleader and student body president. Even then, I'd known she was the kind of person who would never grow out of being a high school cheerleader. She seemed like the type of woman who would marry a prick. But I'd decided to reserve judgment until I could see for myself.

We caught JoAnn as she was loading three teenagers into her Cadillac Escalade. She'd not changed too much since high school, other than putting on about twenty pounds, but the weight had given her a voluptuous appearance in all the right places. Her hair was still white blonde and it was pulled into a high ponytail. And I could understand what Katie meant about modesty. She wore skin tight workout pants with a sheer panel up each leg and a black sports bra with the same sheer paneling. It showed just about everything but her nipples. It was obvious she worked hard for her body, but I wasn't sure if she was going to the gym or about to walk down the Victoria's Secret runway.

"Can we take a minute of your time, JoAnn?" Jack asked as we came around the Escalade.

I saw the annoyance on her face before she looked up and realized who had asked the question.

"Well, well, well," she purred, the voltage of her smile going up a few thousand watts. "If it isn't King George's top cop." She put her hand on a cocked hip and shut the car door so her kids were closed inside. Her nails were freshly manicured and painted bright coral, and her teeth looked especially white against tanned skin.

"I've been keeping up with you," she said. "Who would've thought that Hanover High's Most Likely to Succeed would show up in my driveway. To what do I owe the pleasure?" She drew out the word *pleasure* and left her lips puckered at the end just a little too long.

"We're here to speak to you about Rosalyn McGowen's death," Jack said. "This is my wife, Doctor Graves. She's working on the case with me."

JoAnn's smile dimmed slightly at the introduction, but then she changed tactics and turned to me with sympathy. "Of course I know who you are," she said. "And aren't y'all the cutest crime fighting duo. I was reading about you just this morning. You're so brave. I'm sure Jack appreciates your loyalty. Especially during election season. Voters like for their elected officials to be married. It's never too early to campaign. It's a good idea, doing door to doors together, letting people see the unity."

I'd already had enough of JoAnn Taylor. My bullshit meter could only take so much. "We're actually here about Rosalyn McGowen."

JoAnn sucked in a deep breath. "Of course, of course." Her expression was tragic. "I expected something might have happened to her when I saw the police cars on the way back from my Rotary Club luncheon. I called Janet Selby a couple of doors down and she told me Carl had found her this morning, and that she'd been eaten by her cats. At first I thought Janet had already started drinking her wine, but realized it wasn't three o'clock yet so she must be sober."

"Three o'clock?" I asked.

"She has some rule where she won't drink her daily bottle of wine before three o'clock in the afternoon. Of course, that doesn't stop her from having mimosas at the spa and a Tom Collins when we go to lunch at the club." JoAnn chuckled and shook her head like Janet was an incorrigible child. "But those cats are horrible creatures. They liked to taunt my husband. So I'm not surprised they turned on her."

"She was murdered," Jack said.

"Murdered?" she gasped. JoAnn's hand went to her chest. "That's impossible. No one gets murdered on Foxglove Court. It's the safest neighborhood in all of King George County. Harrison is president of the crime watch."

"You said you didn't see the emergency vehicles until after you got home from Rotary," Jack said. "Why didn't you see them this morning?"

"This was my morning to volunteer at assisted living. I'm quite talented in the kitchen. Not that Roz had anything to do with that. She'd never share one of those damned recipes with me. It's just selfish is what it is. She runs the most successful business in Bloody Mary then sells it, makes a fortune on it, but won't sell the recipes. I'm just trying to give back to the community what she so selfishly took away. I volunteer quite a bit," she said, beaming.

"So if you had her recipes, you'd donate all your baked goods to the places where you volunteer?" I asked.

"Don't be silly," she said, giving me a look like I was gum on the bottom of her shoe. "That would be just plain foolish. But there's a chance for Rosie's to become bigger than she ever dreamed. Television, books..." She shrugged. "But she wouldn't leave that damned house. Some sentiment about her husband and the memories they had there. I doubt she would've been murdered and eaten by her cats if she'd been living in a mansion with a bunch of live-in staff."

"That's very sensitive of you," I said.

"When was the last time you saw her?"

JoAnn put a coral tipped nail to her lips as she thought. "I guess on Sunday. She and Carl brought by some banana bread. But I just tossed it in the trash. We're gluten free in this house. Only healthy living for the Taylors."

"Do you remember seeing anyone unusual around the neighborhood early Monday morning? Maybe a strange car?"

"Actually, there was someone," she said. "I have an eight o'clock spin class on Mondays, and then volunteer at the library. I left here about seven thirty. There was a white van parked right in front of Roz's house. I noticed them because they were putting cones down that side of the street. It looked like they were with the power company or something. They had on coveralls. One of them looked just like

Brad Pitt when he was younger. The *Thelma and Louise* years." She narrowed her eyes in thought. "Do you think he lives here in Bloody Mary? The city would have a list of workers they send out, wouldn't they?"

"Or maybe he was disguised as a worker so he could kill an eighty-five-year-old woman," Jack said, his patience clearly run thin.

"Hmm," she said thoughtfully.

"What about your husband?" I asked. "Is he available to speak with?"

"Honey, Harrison is a very busy man," she said. "He doesn't even have time to speak to me. He's very influential in the community. Of course, you know that, Jack." She batted her eyelashes flirtatiously. "He's devoted his life to this city. He's loved being the DA, but there comes a time when higher aspirations come calling. It's important to be on the right side at that point, don't you think?"

I understood perfectly what the Brights had been saying about Harrison and JoAnn trying to run the neighborhood like he was the president of more than the crime watch. They were bullies, plain and simple. I didn't like bullies.

"Those of us with influence have to support each other. Isn't that right? There's only one chance in an election season. It would be a shame for something to start circulating that could hurt your reputation before the election."

"I'm not worried about that right now," Jack said. His voice had gotten quiet and if I were JoAnn Taylor, I'd be shaking in my boots. The quieter Jack got, the more dangerous he was. "I'm more interested in finding a murderer. But I appreciate the fact that you gave me motive. It seems like killing for those recipes is a likely scenario."

The color drained from her face and Jack handed her a card. "Maybe you could have Harrison give me a call when he gets home or he can stop by and see me at the station. My cell number is on the back. It's possible he might have witnessed something important when he went out with the running club Monday morning."

JoAnn regrouped, but her cheerleader smile didn't reach her eyes this time. "I'm sure if anyone saw anything, it would be Harrison. He's very observant. He's really whipped those runners into shape. When they first started, they could barely walk down the block without passing out. We believe communities need to be healthy in every aspect, and we're just doing our part."

"Bloody Mary is lucky to have you," Jack said. "We don't want to keep you from the rest of the day."

"No worries," she said, waving a hand. "I'm just dropping the kids at various practices and heading to the gym." Her hand went to the door handle, but she didn't open it. "Do you happen to know who's going to get her recipes? She always carried a laptop with her. It was almost as big as she was. Maybe there's a way I could purchase them from the sheriff's office."

"No, ma'am. All electronics and files have been taken in as evidence," he lied. She didn't need to know that the laptop was missing. "It's a murder investigation."

"Right," she said. "Well, I'd love to get together and talk about your upcoming campaign. I've got some great ideas that will really put you over the top come November."

"Jaye and I would love to get together with you," Jack said smoothly. "Maybe the four of us can go to dinner one night. Make sure you tell Harrison to get in touch."

We left JoAnn Taylor looking a little put out and moved out of the driveway so she didn't back over us.

I'd had chills on my skin from the second JoAnn had made the veiled threat of compromising information that could ruin reputations. There was only one person who had that kind of power.

"She's Madam Scandal," I told Jack, grabbing his arm. "She's got to be. She all but admitted it with that jab about people with influence supporting each other during an election. You said it yourself. She's got motive. She wants those recipes. They're worth a fortune. So she kills her, and then threatens you with scandal if you pursue the investigation of her."

"I'm not saying that she couldn't have done it," Jack said. "We'll look into her and Harrison both. Which is going to be fun and a headache all at the same time."

"Madam Scandal knows everyone's secrets in this town," I said. "And she's clearly got political pull. She broke the news of Mayor Walsh's Parkinson's in the KGT this morning. She essentially ruined any chance he had of running for governor. That's the perfect position for someone like JoAnn Taylor to be in. She can do her part to get her husband to the top. You heard her—Harrison has bigger aspirations on his plate. Neither of them seem the kind of person to let a little murder get in the way of something they want."

"All we can do is our jobs by the letter of the law. We're

not going to be intimidated by a blowhard like Harrison Taylor. He knows that about me. So if he's guilty, he should be worried. If he's not guilty, he's still just the asshole he always was. Men like Harrison Taylor can only bully their way into getting what they want for so long. He's taking too many kickbacks and doing too many favors for the wrong people. His day is coming."

"What about the white van?" I asked as we walked to the next house. It was two stories of red brick with a double balcony that had been painted blindingly white. According to Katie, this was Tom and Lynette Miller's house. Hosts of the neighborhood barbecues and owner of the swimming pool.

"I'll put a call in to the city and see if they dispatched someone for this area at that time. But the timeline of their arrival seems a little late to me. Especially if Robert is saying her windows were closed when he got back from his run. It could really narrow the window of time of death."

"Looks like Tom and Lynette aren't home," I said when no one came to the door.

"The Selbys are next," Jack said, checking his list.

We were about to head up Selbys' sidewalk when I saw the blinds flutter in the house next to them. It was a house much like Mrs. McGowen's, but it had a For Sale sign in the front yard. It was the house where the running club met.

"Who lives in that house?" I asked. "I just saw the blinds move."

Jack turned to look at the house in question. Part of it was obscured by the trees, but there was a clear view of the row of windows in the front. We watched for a minute to see if they moved again, but there was nothing.

Jack looked down at his notepad where he'd been collecting information, but it was more out of habit than for information. I knew he'd memorized everything as he was writing it down. He was incredible with details.

"No one's said anything about it other than it's where the running club meets, so I assumed it was vacant. Let's go check it out."

I followed Jack to the front door and used my phone to type in the listing for the house. "Holy cow," I said. "Do you know how much they're trying to sell this thing for? Surely property value hasn't gone up this much in Bloody Mary."

Jack's brows raised when I showed him the price. "Maybe there's gold buried in the basement."

"Hmmmph. Don't say that. It makes me think of my dad." And then a cold frisson of fear washed over me.

It had been a while since I'd heard from my dad. Not since he'd stolen the boxes of flash drives, cash, and IDs from our safe. He'd told me at the time that everything in those boxes was his insurance. That things weren't exactly what they seemed. I couldn't trust him, but I didn't know what to believe. I'd resigned myself to the kind of man he was, or at least I'd told myself I had. But he had to be staying somewhere. Maybe in a place just like this one. Vacant while it waited to be sold.

"We'll check it out," Jack said, clearly reading my mind.

He rang the doorbell twice and then knocked. Nothing. We

waited and strained to listen for any sounds on the other side of the doorway.

"Yoohoo!" A high-pitched voice called out.

We looked over in time to see a woman wobbling her way across the lawn in skyscraper heels and a red power suit. Her dark hair was pulled into a French twist and her lips matched the suit.

"Would you like to see the house?" she asked enthusiastically. "I've already got interested buyers, but if you put in a competitive offer, you could probably beat them to the table."

She found solid footing on the sidewalk and had her hand extended before she even reached us. Something about her made me want to run in the opposite direction.

"Janet Selby," she said, practically grabbing my hand before I had it fully extended. "I'm the listing agent. I saw you walk over and thought I'd come introduce myself. I live next door."

She barely took a breath before she started talking again. I was mesmerized by her energy. It was exhausting. She had big blue Disney eyes and a blindingly white smile.

"You two look very familiar," she said, cocking her head. "Do you have family here? I pride myself on knowing all the founding families. Six generations of Selbys have lived in Bloody Mary."

She moved right past us and used her code to unlock the big key fob that hung around the knob. A key fell into her hand and then she stuck it in the deadbolt, turning it with a decisive click. I looked at Jack and shrugged. We wanted to see if someone had been in the house. This was an easy way to do it. And it wasn't like she'd given us a chance to introduce ourselves.

"The house was built in 1945, but it's been completely renovated and expanded. The structure is solid. I personally think it's the best house on the street, but the couple in the farmhouse across the street would disagree.

"I'll admit the Planters did a great job renovating. That house was falling apart at the seams. But come on," she said conspiratorially. "The whole Chip and Joanna thing is so overdone. Everyone's got barn doors and lamps made of mason jars. You'd think someone with the way and the means to do that kind of renovation work could come up with something more original."

"You don't like the neighbors?" I asked.

Jack moved from room to room, checking for signs of another person. Janet hardly noticed he'd left. It was an open floor plan, but much too modern for my taste. Not that I was house hunting.

Janet had obviously taken the time to make sure the house was ready to show at a moment's notice. The scent of chocolate chip cookies was pumping through the air vents, and freshly cut freesia tied with a red ribbon sat in a tall, skinny vase on the kitchen counter. When I was a kid, we had wild freesia growing along the side of our house, and my mom would tie it with a ribbon before she put it in the vase.

I shook my head, trying to dispel the memory. I knew running from my past wasn't the way to heal, but it never ceased to surprise me when even the smallest reminder of my parents could trigger me into the abyss.

"Oh, it's not like that," she said. "Carl and Robert are lovely people. Very down to earth. Though poor Robert struggles from housewife syndrome, if you know what I mean."

I had no idea what she meant, but I was almost a hundred percent certain that Robert wouldn't like being called a housewife. I raised my brows in question. Getting Janet Selby to talk definitely wasn't a problem.

Jack came back from the bedroom areas and shook his head subtly at me. No one else was in the house.

"Poor thing is bored out of his mind," Janet went on. "Carl is working all the time, and Robert tries to fill his days and nights with endless hobbies. It's only a matter of time before he starts looking for comfort elsewhere. I hope they don't divorce, especially since they were finally able to get married. Seems to defeat the purpose, if you ask me."

No one had asked her anything, but she continued to vomit at the mouth. I wondered if assaulting her client's hearing and holding them hostage was how she got them to sign on the dotted line.

"They had a lovely wedding," she said. "The whole street was invited. Of course, if they did divorce, I'm sure they would come to me to sell the house. We're all very close. We have a neighborhood potluck once a month, we have a running club, and a neighborhood watch. Foxglove Court is one of the safest streets in Virginia."

She walked into the open space and spread her arms. "As you can see, the kitchen, dining, and living area is completely open. It's a great family home. Everything has been modernized and upgraded. And what a great backyard. The pergola and fans alone are a godsend in this heat. And there's plenty of room to put in a pool. Do you have children?"

"Not yet," Jack said, and I felt my face flush. We'd briefly talked about children, as far as the fact that we wanted to have them. Eventually. But that had been the extent of the conversation.

"Mrs. Selby," Jack said.

"Oh, please call me Janet. We're all friends here on Foxglove Court. In fact, we lost one of our own early this morning," she said, her eyes filling with sadness. I had a feeling she was the kind of woman who practiced her expressions in front of a mirror. "It's like losing a family member. She'd lived a good life though, poor thing."

"Janet," Jack tried again and this time he held up his badge. "I'm Sheriff Lawson and this is Doctor Graves. We actually would like to talk to you about Rosalyn McGowen."

"Well, why didn't you say so?" she asked, clearly put out. "I thought you looked familiar. So…what do you think of the house? I heard you've got a place out on Heresy Road. I haven't seen it, but I bet it's spectacular. That's prime real estate overlooking the Potomac. I could get you top dollar for it if you're looking to downsize."

"We're actually happy where we are," Jack said. "Does anyone live here?"

"No," Janet said. She reached down and took off her mega-high heels and then sat on one of the barstools, obviously giving up on the hard sell. "This place has been vacant about six months. The owners won the lottery of all things and they moved to Florida. They don't seem in a hurry to sell and it's a little overpriced for the market, so who knows how long it will take?"

"No one ever uses the house?" Jack asked. "We thought we saw someone inside. That's why we came over."

Janet frowned and rubbed the bottom of her foot. "Only realtors know the key code for the lockbox on the door. And I'd notice any cars parked on the street or strangers walking about the yard. My office faces this house directly, so I've got a good view. Why are y'all here again?"

"Mrs. McGowen," Jack said. "She was murdered. We need to ask you some questions."

She snorted out a half laugh. "Murdered? You're joking. She was an eighty-something year old woman. Why would anyone want to murder her?"

"That's what we're trying to find out. Maybe someone finally found a way to get hold of her recipes."

She *hmmphed* derisively. "You'd want to talk to JoAnn about that. She's as relentless as a pit bull. According to her, those recipes are a gold mine. I personally think JoAnn just finally found someone that could tell her no, and she's bound and determined to get things her way. Sure, maybe the recipes were worth something when the bakery was still open. Rosie had offers for a show on Food Network and bigger corporations wanting to buy her out. But she sold it, and the new place went out of business within the first year. There's nothing valuable there anymore."

"You're part of the running club, aren't you?" Jack asked.

"Sure," she said. "It's important to keep up the image."

"You ran Monday morning?"

"We meet in the front yard here," she said. "I arrived about five-fifteen so I could warm up. Robert and Abby were already here. Everyone else trickled a few minutes after me. We took off shortly after."

"Did you notice any activity at Mrs. McGowen's that morning? Anyone lurking around the house?"

She laughed and then looked at Jack with astonishment when she realized he was serious. "You're serious? You really think she was murdered?"

"She was," I said. "I confirmed it this afternoon. She had signs of blunt force trauma."

"You're saying someone broke in and whacked a little old lady over the head? Over what? Worthless recipes in that computer of hers? That makes no sense. She's right in the middle of the block. Someone would've seen something."

"I hope so. Did you notice anything when you ran by her house?"

"She's an early bird," Janet said. "Always up in the middle of the night. She was that morning, like usual. The woman was batty if you ask me. In bed by eight o'clock. You could set your watch by her. But then she'd just leave and prowl around town in the middle of the night. I think she was having a wild affair. There's no other reason to sneak about like that. It's nice to think a person can be satisfied at that age."

Janet said that last part with just a hint of bitterness, and I wondered how satisfied she was in *her* marriage.

"I tried to talk her into going to one of those retirement communities," she said. "There's no reason for a woman her age to rattle around in a house like that by herself. Anything could've happened. And look, it did." She waved her hands around to bring home the point. "Besides, real estate is prime in this area right now. Speaking of...who inherits her house?" She slipped a card from her jacket pocket and handed it to me. "Have them give me a call once it's all cleaned up. Though murder is never good for selling a house."

"You mentioned a computer," I said.

"It was a laptop. She was pretty paranoid about it—that's why she kept it in a safe when she was gone. She mostly used her phone when she left the house. She was on that thing all the time, and old age didn't slow down her thumbs. She could type faster than any teenager. If you ask me, it was more likely she was messing with the stock market or moving money from accounts than working on recipes. That's just stupid. No recipe is worth that much."

"What do you mean she kept it in a safe?" Jack asked. "We didn't find a safe in her house."

"My husband, Richard, he's a vet, and a couple of years ago he had a real sophisticated safe installed at the clinic to keep the narcotics in. He'd had a couple of break-ins. Rosie asked him to connect her with the same company. It was special made and real expensive, but he said she didn't balk at the price tag. He suggested she go to the bank and get set up with a safety deposit box for her valuables, but she told him no. She said she needed something in her house so she could get things in and out quickly. He thought maybe it was just her being eccentric."

"Do you know where her safe was located?" Jack asked.

"I don't know. Richard connected her to the company, but she was hush hush when it came to the installation. She had it installed a few months ago. I remember they came on Valentine's Day because the florist delivery van was driving up and down the street, delivering flowers left and right. JoAnn Taylor got five dozen white roses, and even little Katie Stein got tulips and one of those tacky balloons."

It was impossible not to hear the bitterness.

"Are you sure she was murdered?" she asked.

"Positive," Jack said. "Did she have any enemies that you knew of?"

"I don't know if *enemies* is the right word," Janet said. "Sometimes she'd complain about this guy down at the senior's center. Hank something or other. They played dominoes and she said he cheated. Apparently they had a pretty heated discussion, and they were both put on probation from the center for a week."

"No one in the neighborhood had problems?" he asked.

She laughed, but it wasn't filled with humor. "Oh, plenty of people in the neighborhood have problems. But mostly everyone got along with Rosie."

"Is your husband at home? I'd like to talk to him."

"Richard left for a conference on Sunday afternoon. He'll be back tomorrow."

"Call me if you can think of anything else?" Jack said, handing her his card. "We'll see ourselves out."

"Let me know if I can help you with any real estate needs. No one in the area can get rid of property like I can. It's a seller's market."

"I'll remember that," Jack said.

My ears were ringing by the time we were back outside. I'd had my fill of people for the day. This was just another one of the reasons I preferred working with the dead.

"Look on the bright side," I said as we made our way back to Mrs. McGowen's house. "I think we can say with certainty that it'll be a cold day in hell before we move to this neighborhood."

"Quarter," Jack said.

"Give me a break. Hell is a location, not a swear word."

"Quarter," he repeated.

# 7

I REALLY DIDN'T WANT TO GO BACK INSIDE ROSALYN McGowen's place, but I knew we needed to see the scene again now that we had new information. There were days I had to take multiple showers because of the hazards of my job. It looked like this was going to be one of them.

I was always well-equipped for a death, so we suited back up and put on fresh booties and gloves. Martinez and Chen were gone, and it was just the two of us at the house. It seemed as if the neighbors had lost interest because I no longer felt eyes on us.

"I'll head over to the senior center later and see if I can find Hank," Jack said, unlocking the front door and letting us inside. He left it open and then immediately went to open some of the windows to let in a draft. He left the windows shut where the curtains had been closed in them. I flipped on the ceiling fan from the light switch in the entryway.

The smell was still bad, but the breeze made it a little more tolerable. Now that there wasn't a body that needed immediate attention, I took a little more time to look around.

"We've got a pretty narrow timeline to work with," Jack said. "Carl walks her back to the door around six. She watches TV for a little while, volume on full blast, and then she's in bed by eight."

The house wasn't large, so it took no time at all to follow her steps into the bedroom. "No one saw her leave the house that night, so we'll assume she slept here. She's an early riser, a habit from her days at the bakery I'm sure. She sleeps on the left side of the bed," he said, pointing to the nightstand. "That's where her personal belongings are. Lamp, phone charger plugged in, planner. Nothing on the other nightstand. Nothing in the drawers.

"She wakes up around four and goes straight to the kitchen," Jack said.

I followed behind him. Seeing it as he saw it.

"It's habit after so many years. Cats twining between her feet as she pushes through to the kitchen. She's making cinnamon rolls so she starts the dough. Practiced moves."

He opened the door of the subzero fridge and then let it go again. Moving around the kitchen, from counter to oven to sink.

"Dough has to rise for cinnamon rolls."

"Seriously, Jack. You don't have to rub it in." I looked around the kitchen and tried to see it without the blood and other things.

I was pretty much useless in the kitchen. Or maybe the

better description was that I was intimidated by the kitchen. I'd excelled in school in math and science, and there were certain things I'd pursued over the years that came easy to me. Cooking was not one of those things, so I tended to avoid it to keep from looking like a fool. Jack, on the other hand, was a miracle in the kitchen.

"Maybe I'll take a cooking class," I said, deciding the best way to get over the fear was to tackle it head on.

"Ummm," Jack said, looking thoroughly confused. Considering we were in the middle of a murder investigation, my announcement probably seemed like it came out of left field.

"Sorry, just a sidebar. Keep going," I said.

"She gets the dough ready and then it's time to feed the cats. They've been waiting while she finished in the kitchen, but it's their turn now."

I followed Jack into the second bedroom that had belonged to the cats. He'd been right. It was ironically cleaner than the rest of the house. There were seven cages stacked against one wall and a giant playground with scratching posts and plenty of things to climb on. Food and water bowls were scattered haphazardly across the floor.

"She comes in and feeds the cats, and then she gets her laptop from the safe and takes it to the little desk in the living room. That's where the neighbors reported seeing her using it. But where is the safe?"

We checked the closet in the cat room, but there were no hollowed out spaces in the walls. Just days' worth of cat food and litter stacked in it.

We went to the master bedroom next and looked behind pictures on the walls, under rugs, and in the freakishly organized closet. Even with the mess the cats had left, it was easy to see where order had reigned in Mrs. McGowen's life. She was extremely organized and efficient.

"Organized and efficient," I said aloud.

"What's that?" Jack asked, knocking on the walls.

"She's organized and efficient. Say she starts every day exactly as you said. She's got a rhythm. A system. And she's older than she used to be, so she doesn't waste time and energy. Bedroom to kitchen. Kitchen to cat room. Cat room to computer."

I left the master bedroom and stood in the small hallway, contemplating the large mirror that had first caught my eye earlier that morning.

Jack saw where I was standing and rubbed his gloved fingers around the outside frame.

"Too high," I said. "She was right at sixty-four inches in height." I moved to the left side of the mirror and ran my fingers along the bottom corner. It didn't take long to feel the slight bump along the metal frame.

I pushed the button and the mirror opened from the wall with a soft *click*.

"There we go," Jack said, swinging it open all the way. Behind the mirror was a safe no bigger than a microwave. "Now we just need to get it open."

"It's got a numerical passcode," I said. "Other than trying

her birthday or something like that, I'm at a loss on how to open it. Unless you want to blow it up."

"I'll have the team come in and cut it out of the wall. Once it's back at the station, I'll call the manufacturer and send them the warrant. They'll have an override code we can use."

"Huh," I said. "I can see why they pay you the big bucks. That seems a lot simpler than blowing it up. But not near as much fun."

"We can blow up stuff another time, baby. You do bring a whole new level of excitement to date night though. I always feel like I need to up my life insurance."

"A little fear is healthy," I said.

"Good call on the efficiency," he said. "Feed the cats, open the safe, and take the computer to the desk. Maybe she'd turn the TV on while she's working on whatever it is she does on that computer. From witness testimony, you're looking at a TOD between five-thirty when the runners took off, and around seven when they started to return. I need to talk to Harrison Taylor. He made it back before anyone else. No matter what time he returned, that's a really small window of opportunity to kill Mrs. McGowen, close the windows, and then escape without being seen. It would've had to have been someone very familiar with her schedule and habits."

"Meaning someone who lives close enough to watch her every day," I said. "Maybe Harrison got back early enough to do the job himself. Then he just jogs home and showers."

"Then the question is, what kind of information would someone like Rosalyn McGowen have for someone as powerful as Harrison Taylor to feel threatened?"

"You really should talk to him," I said, repeating his earlier statement.

Jack squeezed the back of my neck. "Good idea, babe." We walked back out onto the front porch and the fresh air made my eyes sting. "I'm going to wait here for the guys so we can get this safe out of the wall and to the conference room, and then I'm going to stop by the senior center."

"I'll go by the funeral home and check on things there," I said. "I need to look at the head wound and see if I can get a viable mold."

He leaned down to kiss me hard and quick. "Don't be too long. We've got a date with some steaks."

# 8

I WAS PROBABLY THE ONLY PERSON IN A HUNDRED-MILE radius who actually enjoyed the solitude of the funeral home once everything had shut down. This was a place of sanctuary for the dead. It wasn't meant for ringing phones and difficult decisions. It wasn't meant for the problems of the living. Once we closed down for the day, the dead in residence could have their peace.

There was no viewing scheduled for the evening, so Emmy Lu had shut things down at five o'clock. I parked under the covered awning and went through the side door. But I bypassed the lab, going straight into the kitchen to grab a bottle of water. I was jumpy, and I realized it was because I'd had nothing but coffee and unlimited amounts of sweet tea all day.

After I grabbed the water, I went into the main reception area. The idea of the funeral home was to make it feel like a home when people came to visit their loved ones for the last time. The entryway was warm and inviting, and the theme of soft blues and creams carried up into the upper levels, accented with the occasional hint of navy in a chair or other upholstered piece.

We didn't have a reception desk right in front. Only a wooden stand where a sign in book would go for each family. Emmy Lu's office was set back a little ways in a cove off to the side. That way people didn't think "business" the second they walked in. It was glass on two sides so she could see anyone who came in.

The door was open and I walked in to see if there were any messages and to check the board. Mrs. Richardson's husband hadn't passed yet, and even if he did tonight or tomorrow, we were probably looking at Monday at the earliest for a viewing. Sheldon was on call to collect the body once the hospital called and let us know he'd passed.

The calendar on the wall looked healthy, and I breathed out a sigh of relief. One of my biggest fears was hiring employees and then having to let them go because the business wasn't sustaining. Whether people were coming in to buy burial plans or doing like Mrs. Richardson and waiting, at least people were coming in.

I grabbed a peppermint off Emmy Lu's desk and made my way back to the lab and Mrs. McGowen's bones. I typed in the code and then closed the door behind me, opting for the stairs again.

Lily had done a good job of laying her out. The break in the right ulna had been clean and the two halves of the bones were lined up in place to make up the skeleton. But it was the trauma to the skull I was interested in.

I'd thought I'd be able to get a good mold of the head wound, but there was nothing I could do with it. I wasn't a forensic anthropologist and it was far out of my depth of knowledge. The wound wasn't a spider fracture, meaning the initial indentation where the object struck made a crater like indent and then fissures spidered outward. I was guessing she'd have pretty severe osteoporosis at her age, and when the object had struck bone, it had shattered that part of the skull. Little pieces of the parietal sat next to the skull on the table.

I tossed my gloves in the trash and hung up my apron. There was nothing more I could do there tonight. The evidence they'd collected would have to be enough to find her killer because her body was staying silent.

---

I LOVED GOING HOME. There was something about driving around that last curve, the road widening slightly and the trees opening up, and into the hidden entrance of our driveway. Gravel crunched under my tires, and I saw Jack's unit parked in front of the closed garage doors. We kept our personal vehicles inside, but they rarely move from that space.

Jack had designed the log cabin, though calling it a log cabin didn't do it justice. It was three stories of polished golden logs. A covered porch wrapped around the entire bottom. There were no windows in the front by design, because when you stepped inside, it was like the house was part of the cliff it was built on. The entire back of the house was nothing but glass. The towering pines and rocks could be seen from every room, and they looked as if they were part of the décor.

I unlocked the front door and felt the tension leave my shoulders. The house was still, the hush of quiet overwhelming as I tossed my keys in the little bowl on the entry table. The kitchen was empty, so I headed upstairs, bypassing the second floor.

The entire third floor was the master suite, and I immediately kicked off my shoes and changed out of my clothes. I could see Jack out on the balcony, putting steaks on to grill. He'd already showered and put on a pair of gray sweats and a T-shirt. He had a beer in his hand and his earbuds in, and I could see his mouth was moving. He was on the phone with someone.

I chucked my clothes in the hamper and turned on the water in the walk-in shower to blistering hot. Steam billowed out of the open doorway. I didn't linger, but washed quickly and then turned off the water. I grabbed the towel from the rod and dried off, wrapping the towel around my head while I went in search of clothes. I opted for gray sweats like Jack's and an old U of V T-shirt that was threadbare in places.

I hung the towel back over the rod and ran fingers through wet hair, deciding to let it dry on its own. I opened the sliding glass door from our bedroom and stepped out onto the balcony, inhaling the fresh scent of trees and listening to the water of the Potomac rush against the rocks below.

Jack was just hanging up the phone when I walked over to him. He put an arm around my waist and I leaned into him, kissing him hello.

"Mmm," he said. "Hello to you too." And he kissed me again, a little longer, a little deeper this time.

When I pulled back, my heart was pounding in my chest, and I knew if we kept going the steaks would end up forgotten. There was a small outdoor kitchen on the balcony outside of our bedroom and a table and two chairs. There were heat lamps for the winter and fans for the summer. We spent a lot of time outdoors. The large patio with an upscaled and upsized version of everything was for entertaining others, but this space was just for us.

I went to the small fridge built into the kitchen and got out a bottle of wine. I knew we had work left to do, but one glass would hit the spot. Jack handed me a glass and I poured generously.

"That was Nash on the phone," he said. "The safe is locked in the conference room. We'll call the manufacturer in the morning for the override code."

"Maybe whoever killed her didn't get the laptop," I said. "Maybe they didn't know about the safe."

"You really think Janet Selby was able to keep that secret?" he asked.

No, I didn't think so. I wasn't sure anyone on that street would be able to keep a secret if you sewed all their mouths shut.

Jack flipped the steaks and my mouth watered as they sizzled. The day was starting to catch up to me.

"Things aren't looking good for someone on Foxglove Court," I said. "They knew her habits, her schedule, her potential worth, and they knew she had a safe. Makes it almost improbable for it to be a random killing. Especially when you factor in time of death."

"No," Jack agreed. "We need to look deeper."

He put each of the steaks onto a plate, and then pulled a salad bowl from the fridge. I could've done without the salad, but Jack liked a balanced meal. And I could always drown it in dressing. I carried the salad bowl to the table along with my wine and then went back for the plates while Jack dealt with the grill.

We both dug in and I was about to swallow the first, delicious bite when Jack said, "You looked like you might pass out when Janet asked if we had kids."

"Technically, that's not true. I almost passed out when you said not yet."

He chuckled and took a swig of beer. "Touché. Do kids scare you?"

"I don't know," I said, shrugging. "I've not been around any. But this conversation kind of scares me."

"It's not like we're going to have a baby right now," he said.

I took a drink of wine. And kept drinking.

"Relax, Jaye. There's no hurry or pressure. You want kids someday, right?"

"Right," I said, letting out the breath I'd been holding.

"Me too. But not right now. We've got some years for just the two of us before we bring someone else into the mix."

I cut my steak into little pieces, but didn't put any into my mouth. "What if I'm not good at it?" I asked. "Having kids, I mean."

Jack stared at me from across the table. He was so handsome. His face backlit by the waning sunlight. Dark eyes that could always see the real me, even when I tried to hide.

"Why would you think that?" he asked. "You're amazing. You have more kindness and compassion than anyone I've ever met. Look what you do for people you've never met before, and for the dead that are brought to you. You'll be an amazing mother when the time comes."

"I don't know how to be that," I said. "Look how I was raised. Look *who* raised me."

"Bullshit," he said, leaning closer across the table. "Your parents and how they raised you means nothing in this. Because you had good parents. My mom and dad, for example. Vaughn's parents. Hell, even Mrs. McGowen. You'll never be what your parents were. I have no doubt in my mind."

I felt tears prick my eyes and looked down at my plate, hurriedly putting a bite in my mouth.

When we finished, Jack stood and took my plate and put everything in the sink. I still wasn't used to having a housekeeper. I'd never had one my entire life, and I spent most of my time cleaning things up before Molly came so she wouldn't think we were complete slobs.

"Come on," he said, pulling me to my feet. "We've got work to do."

"Have you started on the board yet?" I asked.

Jack was visual and needed to lay out all the information on the murder board before the pieces started falling into place. Before we were through, we'd know everything about everyone on Foxglove Court.

"No, not yet," he said. "But that's not what I meant about having work to do." He kissed the side of my neck, and chills pebbled on my skin.

"Jack..."

"Ssh," he said, turning me in his arms and kissing the corner of my mouth before planting his lips squarely on mine. I sighed and leaned into him.

"But what about work?"

He backed me slowly toward the bedroom and through the sliding glass door.

"I'll be quick," he said. He pulled the shirt over my head and released the drawstring on my sweats.

"Not too quick, I hope."

He chuckled against my neck and fell back with me on the bed. "Not too quick. I promise."

# 9

BY THE TIME WE GOT DRESSED AND DOWNSTAIRS, IT WAS A little after nine o'clock.

It was weird having such a big house with only the two of us living there. There were several rooms that went unused —spare bedrooms, the music room, the formal dining room. When we had company, it was close friends or Jack's mom, and we weren't formal about anything, so those rooms usually had the doors closed. And neither of us played the piano, and no one wanted to hear me sing, so that door remained closed as well.

That wasn't the case for the office. It was a masculine room, more so than the other rooms in the house, but I loved it. The floor was hand scraped wood, the furniture was leather, and heavy wooden beams supported the ceiling. A big stone fireplace sat in the middle of the wall facing the door—an imposing statement—and floor to ceiling windows flanked each side. The electric shades were pulled down over the windows, but in the daytime, it showed the view of the trees.

It was a peaceful room, and I liked to come in and read in one of the oversized chairs in front of the fireplace, even when the fire wasn't on. The wall adjacent to the fireplace was floor-to-ceiling bookshelves, and there wasn't any space left. Jack had always been a big fiction reader, and his tastes were eclectic—from Steve Berry to JD Robb—and he didn't care that the books weren't all hardback first editions. Many of the paperbacks had cracked spines from been read so often. I'd always been a big non-fiction and academic journal reader, but we'd had a lot of time to do nothing but relax on our honeymoon, and I'd found myself devouring one novel after another.

There was a rectangular table with no chairs, and a desk with a desktop and a laptop on it. Behind the desk was the giant map of King George County Vaughn had talked about. To the side was a large white board.

The process of creating a murder board was time consuming, but the visualization was necessary. I'd learned after my first investigation that the things people said got confusing after a while.

"Can you sing?" I asked Jack randomly. I'd known him my whole life and never remembered hearing him sing.

He looked a little startled by the question, and stared at me with brows raised. "I can't even imagine what spurred you to ask that question."

We had printed photographs of everyone in the neighborhood and we were placing them in order of where each person lived on the street.

"I was just thinking about the music room," I said. "We never go in there. No one plays the piano. It's just weird."

"I play the piano," he said, putting up Robert and Carl's photos.

"I'm sorry, what?" My mouth dropped open in surprise. "How can that be?"

"I took lessons as a kid. I just don't play often anymore. Honestly, I forget we even have a piano."

"Do Vaughn and Dickey know you play?" I asked, eyes narrowed.

"Not that I know of." He grinned at me and put up another picture. "I always told them I had a golf lesson every Thursday. Piano lessons didn't go with my image."

"Lies," I whispered. "A web of lies. Are you telling me you don't golf? All these years I thought you were some golf pro hotshot."

"I hate golf," he said. "I don't have the patience for it. Never took a lesson in my life. I was just less embarrassed about golf than I was about piano. What did I know? I was eight. And then I was fourteen and I *really* didn't want anyone to know. If I'd known earlier how much women love musicians, I would've played in public all the time."

"You've never played for me," I said, hands on hips.

"No need to impress you now. We're married."

I tossed a pen at his head and he ducked, laughing.

"You're going to play for me at some point. It's one of those marriage rules. No secrets. And don't think I haven't noticed you changed the subject away from your singing."

"The fact that I changed the subject to something no one

around here knows about but my mother should be a pretty good indicator of how well I sing."

"I guess you have a point."

Once the pictures were up, Jack started making a timeline of events.

"Did you get the report from Chen and Martinez?" I asked.

"Yeah, I looked over it briefly. It's in my email if you want to print it out."

I opened the laptop and logged into his email, and then I scrolled down until I saw the attachment from Martinez.

"What happened at the senior center?" I asked.

"About what you could expect," he said. "In my experience, seniors don't get too excitable about death. Especially past a certain point. And they certainly don't hold back what they're thinking. George Martin told me he'd miss the homemade donuts, and Helen Brubaker told me she'd finally have a chance at winning at dominoes now that Roz was gone."

"What about the infamous Hank?"

"He admitted that he and Rosalyn had gotten into it a time or two, but he said he was really sorry to hear that someone had gone and murdered her. And then he followed it up by saying he wasn't surprised because she was a she-devil in disguise."

"So depending on who you talk to, Mrs. McGowen was a saint or a sinner."

"Hank's exact words were that she baked like an angel, but was as mean as the devil. But he would miss the old girl."

"Sounds like love to me," I said, shaking my head.

"What we've got is an eighty-five-year-old woman who was financially comfortable and loved by everyone. She's got no next of kin. We've got the search warrants for her bank accounts and life insurance beneficiaries, as well as her will, so we should have all of that in the morning. Without family, it's anyone's guess who she's left things to.

"We know she was murdered in the early morning hours of Monday. Sometime between five and seven o'clock, give or take a half hour. There's always the possibility she was already dead before the members of the running club took off. The killer could have been inside the house as they were running by."

I looked down at the printed report. "We've got a street of thirteen houses. It's a diverse street—Hispanic, black, white, gay, single, old, young, kids, no kids, financial struggles and prosperity. Nine of the houses are married couples. Three of the houses—Mrs. McGowen, Abby Clearwater, and Doug Roland—are singles. One house is vacant. Four houses have school-aged children. Katie, Robert, and Frank and Edna Bright are home consistently during the day. JoAnn Taylor is a wildcard since she volunteers at various places, but her schedule is flexible. Plus, she's a real…jerk."

"She's nothing compared to Harrison," Jack said. "I'd rather have a root canal while having a prostate exam than have to talk to him tomorrow. He's going to make our lives hell."

"How come you get to swear?" I asked. "That's not fair."

"I'm a cop. We're supposed to swear. Besides, hell is a place, not a swear word."

"Hilarious," I said, narrowing my eyes, remembering I'd said the same thing to him earlier.

"What about Tom and Lynette Miller? Aren't they retired?"

"Tom has said he was going to retire for several years, but he still rents an office in the city complex. He's doing taxes for most of the businesses in Bloody Mary. Lynette started working part-time at the pharmacy once her kids graduated high school several years back. We still need to talk to them, but my mom said they make frequent trips to Atlantic City, so they're gone at least one long weekend a month. And apparently, Lynette is a frequent attendee at the bingo hall. They've got two grown children, but both live out of state."

"You talked to your mom today?" I asked.

"She called on my way home. She asked if we wanted to come for dinner Sunday."

My lips twitched. "She wanted to find out about Mrs. McGowen?"

"That too," he said, smiling. Jack grabbed a red marker and turned his attention back to the board. "The running club is consistent, so let's start with that. They meet at the same time, same place, on Monday, Wednesday, and Friday. Monica Middleton, Jenson Davis, Abby Clearwater, Janet Selby, Harrison Taylor, and Robert Planter.

"According to Robert, Harrison never stays with the group.

He's back well before the others, so that leaves him unaccounted for during the window of Mrs. McGowen's murder. Robert, Abby, and Janet all run together, and then Monica and Jenson bring up the rear."

I flipped through the pages of Martinez's report. "Martinez said Monica and Jenson did about a mile and a half total and got back to their respective houses before seven. Monica has to be at the hospital by eight o'clock, so she has to get back in time to shower and change. Jenson owns the State Farm agency in King George."

"Yeah," Jack said. "But I heard he's opening a branch in Bloody Mary in that shopping center across from the funeral home."

"Huh," I said. "It's becoming a downright respectable street since you busted Denny Kasowski."

"Don't think I don't hear the judgment in your tone," he said.

"I'm just saying, the man was doing a service to the community. With the price of insurance and drugs, it was helpful to be able to get my birth control pills for less than ten dollars a month. And I have a full six-month supply."

"Which makes me feel so much better that you've been using discount birth control pills. They could be rat poison for all you know."

"I haven't gotten pregnant, have I?" I said, hands on hips.

"No, and you're not going to either because I'm not touching you again until you throw those away and go to a real doctor."

We'd started out joking, but I could feel my blood pressure elevating. I wasn't good at being told what to do. And I really didn't react well to ultimatums.

"I'm sorry…what did you just say?" I took a step forward and the scar on Jack's eyebrow turned white. "I thought you wanted to have children."

"I also want to have children not hopped up on whatever drugs are in your system. I can't even believe we're having this conversation."

"Denny was a doctor. He had access to real medicine and he helped a lot of people. How many senior citizens have died because they couldn't afford their meds since you arrested him?"

"First of all, Denny was a veterinarian. Second of all, I'm going to pretend like you're not completely off your rocker right now and focus on the murder at hand."

"Oh, instead of all the murders of the elderly not getting their meds?"

"Name one person who's died because of Denny's arrest." Jack said.

I hated it when Jack got mad. He got quieter and his tone more reasonable. It drove me insane. Even when he was wrong, and I'm not saying one way or the other whether he was wrong this time, he presented himself in a way that made him look right.

"Glenda Murkowski," I said.

"Glenda Murkowski was a hundred years old and died in

the nursing home," Jack said, his expression incredulous. "How did Denny's arrest affect her?"

"Mrs. Murkowski was the picture of health. Denny came to visit her once a month and kept her stocked for her heart and blood pressure meds because the nursing home would sometimes forget to give them to her. They're overstaffed and underpaid, so that happens all the time. Denny gets arrested and Glenda is dead a week later."

"What was cause of death?" Jack asked.

"Cardiac arrest." I wasn't about to add that she'd been watching the Yankees, Red Sox game at the time.

"Stop being so hardheaded and stop taking the damned pills. You're a doctor, why can't you write your own prescriptions?"

"Because I'm not practicing anymore," I said. "Dead people typically don't need medicine. And even though Denny was a vet, he was still registered with the DEA for be able to write prescriptions. If he'd stuck to selling birth control pills and penicillin, he would've never gotten caught. Besides, you think I'm dumb enough to take those pills without examining them first?"

Jack sighed, letting a breath out long and slow, and he closed his eyes. "No, I don't think you're dumb. I'm sorry."

I felt the tension and anger drain from my body. "The good news is since we've gotten married, I can actually have health insurance now. If I'd known how cheap it was through the county instead of private pay, I would've married you years ago."

"Hilarious," Jack said, straight-faced. "If I'd known what a huge tax deduction we'd get for being married, I'd have married you years ago too. Are we done with this fight?"

"I haven't decided yet," I said. "But it's probably best we had sex earlier."

"Duly noted."

"Do you think Jenson could be the man Monica is having an affair with?" I asked.

"I guess anything is possible, but you'd think one of the other neighbors would have picked up on it. It's hard for two people to hide it when they have a sexual relationship. People *think* they do a good job of concealing it, but there are little things that give it away. Robert said it was for Monica's protection. Because Harrison is such a letch. At least that story is consistent."

"True," I agreed. "Everyone hates Harrison. You'd think he'd be the one who was murdered instead of sweet Mrs. McGowen."

"It's a secluded, cul-de-sac neighborhood," Jack said. "I walked the perimeter today. Behind the houses on Mrs. McGowen's side of the street is nothing but woods. The other side takes you to Galliard Street, but it's a heck of a walk."

"And that's a busy street. You couldn't exactly park on the side of the road without someone noticing."

"Maybe not at that time of the morning, but there are quite a few businesses across the street. Maybe someone has an outdoor camera."

"What's on the other side of the street?" I asked.

"More woods and a creek," he answered. "It's a shorter distance to the nearest street, but it'd be more difficult to get to. The creek is a good twenty feet down, and the terrain is rocky and rough. It wouldn't be easy in the daytime, much less when it was still dark outside."

"Plus, they'd have to make their way to the other side of the street somehow. With the running club out and about, it'd be risky."

"Monica's husband was still on shift and didn't get home until around eight. Nash already checked him out. Clark and Maria Green were asleep. They both were up to start their day around seven. Maria still has pretty bad morning sickness, and she told Martinez that Clark brought her tea and toast to help settle her stomach. Clark got ready for work and left a little after eight. He's an electrician. Maria didn't have to be at work until ten, so she stayed in bed a little longer. She's a manager at the shoe store on Purgatory Drive."

"I love that place," I said. "They're having a BOGO sale right now."

"Good, you should go and talk to her. See what she knows about everyone."

"The silent part of that sentence was that I should buy shoes so I have a good reason to be there."

"You're so good at hearing the things I don't say," he said, his smile tight.

"Marriage is an amazing thing."

"Uh huh," he said. "Jenson and Angela Davis are next door to the Clarks. Jenson was running with Monica. Angela was asleep until she heard Jenson come back home and get in the shower. They have two young kids, and Jenson drops them off at daycare on his way to the insurance agency. Angela is a fitness instructor at the gym. She teaches the eight o'clock spin class that JoAnn Taylor was in.

"Then there's Abby Clearwater. She's in the running group with Robert and Janet. She said she enjoys every minute of her summer break she can. After they got back from their run, she hopped in the shower and then got back in bed. She said she didn't wake up again until after ten. She does work part-time in the afternoons at the florist, but only Monday through Thursday. She likes to have her weekends free. She's got a guy she's been seeing in Richmond."

"Did she have anything to say about Harrison?" I asked.

"Nothing other than he creeped her out," Jack said.

"Too bad there wasn't a Most Likely to Creep Women Out award when we were in high school. Does he have any sexual misconduct complaints?"

"Complaints, yes," Jack said. "But nothing that ever stuck. Mostly from the law clerks and interns who've had the misfortune of working with him. He's got too much money and can make life miserable for anyone who wants to challenge him. At least most people. Women typically steer clear of him."

"Which is ridiculous," I said, my anger going to full throttle. "The fact that women have to just 'stay out of his way' shouldn't be the norm for making his behavior seem acceptable."

"I agree with you," he said. "But until someone comes forward and fights, we can't do anything about it."

I hated it, but he was right. I hadn't given two thoughts to Harrison Taylor since high school, but to find out he'd been terrorizing the women in town made me wish we'd crossed paths.

"Janet Selby is alibied with the running club," he went on. "And Richard left the day before to go to a veterinary conference in DC."

"He could commute that," I said.

"Apparently, this is an annual thing. He goes for the entire week, does business, and meets up with some golfing buddies. We called the hotel and confirmed he checked in on Sunday at three o'clock. The Selbys have two kids, but one's in junior high and the other in high school, so they stay at home in the summer while their parents work.

"Coming up the other side of the street is Doug Roland, and no one has been able to vouch for his whereabouts. He was home Sunday, according to Carl, because he answered the door when they delivered the banana bread. But Katie said he was rarely at home, and no one remembers seeing his car in the driveway the rest of the week. We're still trying to track him down. We did run a background on him, and he's career military. Lives a pretty quiet life. Never married. No children. No debt. No big expenses. Not a gambler. His biggest expense is for a hunting lodge in South Carolina. There's no cell or internet service there, so I'll put in a call tomorrow to the sheriff there and see if they can run him down.

"Katie and Jeremy are next door to Doug. Both of them

were home and asleep since they had a sick kid up all night. But Katie did witness the mystery man at Monica's around midnight."

I scanned through the pages of Martinez's report until I found Monica's statement. "She told Martinez and Chen that she was alone that night. That her husband was at work and she went to bed around ten because she had to get up so early."

"We'll follow back with her on that," Jack said. "Katie's husband went in late that morning because of the sick kid. Mrs. McGowen is next door to them. And then there's Carl and Robert Planter. They both left the house right around five o'clock. Carl to head off to the job site and Robert to walk across the street to the empty house to warm up in the yard."

"The next person to arrive was Janet Selby around five-fifteen," I said. "Robert had fifteen minutes of time alone."

"Yeah, but it's a stretch. He'd have to run across the street, kill her, and be back in place by the time Janet showed up because she said he was already there when she arrived. And they all said that her windows were open when they left and were closed when they returned. Frank and Edna Bright were asleep, and though they're mean as snakes, they're not exactly in the best physical condition to commit murder. And I can't imagine them being quiet enough to get the job done."

I snickered at that. I could imagine the two of them sniping at each other while trying to commit murder.

"That leaves JoAnn and Harrison Taylor. Harrison started with the running club, but he didn't finish with them.

According to JoAnn, he was always back long before the others. She saw him briefly before she left for her spin class. They've got the three kids, but they're all old enough to hang out on their own in the summer."

"So what you're telling me is that out of everyone who lives on that street, Harrison Taylor is the only one who doesn't have an alibi for the window of time we think Mrs. McGowen was murdered in."

Jack nodded and let out an audible breath. "Yep, that's what I'm telling you."

# 10

I GENERALLY WASN'T A MORNING PERSON, BUT AFTER Jack's alarm went off and he got in the shower, I couldn't make myself go back to sleep. But not for lack of trying. In my opinion, people shouldn't get out of bed if it was still dark outside.

My mind wouldn't shut off, so I dragged myself up and into the shower. I dressed in my typical work attire of comfortable black slacks and a black and white striped sleeveless shirt. I grabbed a black cardigan at the last second because the police station was always cold and so was the funeral home.

By the time I got downstairs, Jack was finishing up his breakfast. He handed me a cup of already prepared coffee, and I took a small sip to test the temperature. It was perfect.

"Thank you," I said, my voice croaking.

Several months before, I'd been choked to the point of unconsciousness by a serial killer. My voice had never quite regained its original timbre. It tired easily, and sometimes I'd be hoarse at the end of a long day. And it took a while to warm up in the mornings. But even when I was warmed up, I still had a rasp that had never been there before. Jack told me it was sexy. I tried to believe him.

"I'll see you at the nine o'clock briefing," he said and kissed me on the top of the head. "I've got a meeting at eight, so I've got to get going, but I'm going to try and pin down Harrison Taylor for a meeting at some point today."

"Fun," I said, clearing my throat. "Don't forget Vaughn's coming tonight for dinner."

"Right," Jack said. "Y'all are going to track down the infamous Madam Scandal."

"Hey, maybe if we can find her, she can tell us who killed Mrs. McGowen."

"Very funny," Jack said. "Nine o'clock." And then the front door closed behind him.

I finished my first cup of coffee, enjoying the silence, but there had been something bothering me about Foxglove Court that I couldn't get out of my mind. I had plenty of time before the nine o'clock briefing, so I poured a to-go cup and grabbed my bag before heading out to the Suburban.

I drove into town and then turned onto Galliard Street. Traffic was heavy at this time of the morning, so I had plenty of time to check out the wooded area to my right. Across the street were a few businesses, so someone could have parked there and walked across. And Jack was right—at that time of the morning, there would hardly be anyone out and about. The trees were so thick you couldn't see a hint of the houses behind them.

I circled around to the other side and wound through the neighborhood that backed up to the side of the street the Middletons and Abby Clearwater lived on. It was more of a winding road, and again, the trees were thick. There was also a chain-link fence that ran the length of the trees, presumably protecting people from the powerlines. And there was also a creek that ran somewhere behind the houses. It wouldn't have been impossible to park along this street and make it to Foxglove Court. It was low-end housing and there were more cars parked on the street. Making it over the fence and across the twenty foot drop where the creek ran would have been possible for someone in semi-decent shape. It was just much more complicated for someone to come in that way to kill a little old woman who lived in the middle of the block on the opposite side of the street.

When looking at means, motive, and opportunity, we didn't have a whole lot to go on. We didn't have a suspect, but Harrison Taylor was high on the list of persons of interest. He definitely had the means and opportunity. But what was the motive? Recipes? Maybe if he was doing it for his wife, but in that case, they'd be in on it together. Which I wasn't totally turned off by.

But just because I wanted it to be Harrison or JoAnn didn't mean it was. Everyone else on the street had an alibi. And one of the first things Jack had taught me was to not make things too complicated. Sometimes the simplest answer was, in fact, the right answer.

What if someone had parked along this street, but hadn't

trampled through the woods in the middle of the night? What if they were already on the street, waiting for the right opportunity?

I drove back out of the neighborhood and made my way to Foxglove Court. I parked in front of Mrs. McGowen's house, but that wasn't my focus. I waved to Katie next door as I got out of the Suburban. She was in her usual place by the front window. Doug's truck was still gone, as was Carl's. In fact, the street looked deserted except for Katie's Mazda CX-5 and a dark blue Honda Civic that was parked in the driveway at the Middleton's. I assumed it belonged to Monica's husband, Keith. He'd probably just gotten home from work and was going to bed.

There was still crime scene tape on the front door of Mrs. McGowen's, and I decided to walk up the street and cross by the cul-de-sac because it was harder for Katie to see what I was doing.

I hadn't been dreaming when I'd seen that curtain move in the vacant house the day before. What if the killer had been on the street all along? As soon as the runners took off, they'd be clear to make their way to Mrs. McGowen's house. Her windows were already open. All he'd have to do is remove one of the bedroom screens and slip in. She was hard of hearing anyway, so if her TV was up loud, she wouldn't have heard him enter. Then he bashes her in the head, takes her computer, closes all the windows, and is back outside long before Harrison Taylor comes back from his run. The killer could've stayed in the house all week, waiting and watching to see if someone would discover his handiwork.

And if I was honest, I couldn't get that freesia tied with a ribbon out of my head. It could have been a coincidence, but then again, I wasn't sure I believed in coincidences when it came to my father.

I sent a quick glance toward Janet Selby's house, not wanting to get caught in another conversation, but the driveway was empty. I walked right up to the front door and tried the knob, but it was locked. I rang the bell, just in case, but I didn't hear anything stirring on the inside. The good thing about these houses was that none of them were divided by fences. Most people got their privacy like Mrs. McGowen, by planting hedges or some other kind of plant. But there was nothing that enclosed the vacant house's backyard, though it was more heavily treed than the other lots.

The backyard was nice, and I personally thought Janet should have spent a little more time trying to sell us on those features. There was a covered porch and an outdoor fireplace, and a deck that looked like it was meant for entertaining. And she'd been right—there was plenty of room for someone to add in a pool. If I were to buy a house like this one, the first thing I'd do was make the entire back of the house windows so I could see outside. As it was, there were two windows that sat fairly close together and looked into the living room. The back door was solid and plain.

But when I tried the door knob, it turned beneath my hand, and I felt my pulse start to race. I pushed the door open gently and decided to bluster my way through, just in case there was someone inside. And if there was, hopefully that person wasn't a killer.

"Hello," I said. The sound of my voice echoed back at me.

"I'm just here to look at the house again. Janet said it was okay to come on over. She left the back door unlocked for me."

I waited again, but there was nothing, and I breathed out a sigh of relief. The chocolate chip cookie smell was still wafting through the air, and the house had an empty feel to it. I bypassed the kitchen and went to the front bedroom, where I'd seen the curtains move the day before.

It was a small room, probably used as an office or spare bedroom. The carpet was beige and the walls had been recently painted a soft eggshell. There were no blinds in the window, only the starch-pressed sateen curtains. I touched them, peeking out to the front yard. They were heavy, and there was no way the air conditioning kicking on would have moved them that much.

"You were always a curious child," a voice said from behind me. "Did you notice the freesia? I thought it was a nice touch."

I felt my shoulders tense immediately and took a second to compose my face before I turned around. He'd always moved quietly, like a ghost. I hadn't seen my father since before Jack and I got married. In fact, the last time I'd seen him, Jack had been holding a gun on him, ready to arrest him and turn him back over to the FBI. But no one captured Malachi Graves. Not unless he wanted them to. And just like that, he'd been gone...*pfft*...like a ghost.

"Yes," I said. "And you always told me not to ask too many questions."

"It didn't stop you from asking them," he said, smiling slightly.

He'd changed subtly over the past months, since he'd come back from the dead to haunt the living again. He was a man who could look like anyone, blend in anywhere. He was average height and average build. His hair had been the color of a deer pelt the last time I'd seen him, but he'd dyed it gray with a little bit of silver at the temples, and his goatee matched. He'd gotten rid of the tortoiseshell glasses and was wearing pale blue contacts. His jeans and Henley were nondescript, unmemorable, but he was still my father.

"You know I'm just going to call Jack and tell him where you are," I said.

I didn't bother to try and move past him. He'd let me go whenever he was ready. Malachi had a way of showing up when he wanted something. I doubted I'd have ever seen him again if we hadn't taken a few of his precious flash drives.

"I know," he said, his smile never wavering. He had a charm about him, my dad, that could almost make you forget he was a murderer at worst, a traitor at best. "But I wanted to see you now that you're a married woman. I wished I could've walked you down the aisle."

"There would've been cops falling all over themselves to arrest you," I said. "It would've taken the attention off me a bit."

He laughed like we were talking about something as simple as the weather. "I'm proud of you and Jack, I hope you know that. I always thought the two of you would be good for each other. That maybe you could heal each other."

"Don't…" I said, shaking my head. I felt the tears prick at the corner of my eyes, but I was determined to hold them back. The fact that he'd known how much healing I had to do spoke volumes. My parents had been selfish bastards, and I'd been a convenient side-effect of their cover.

"Everything is not as it seems, Jaye. Your mother and I, we weren't the best parents, but that didn't mean we didn't love you. But we had obligations that had to be finished long before you came into the picture. If we'd stopped what we were doing, you wouldn't be alive to have that newlywed glow about you. In fact, a lot of people would be dead."

"People are already dead," I said. "Who's to say who should still be alive? It's not like I can trust that you're on the side of the good guys."

He sighed and stuck his hands in his pockets, jingling the change there. He used to do that when he was thinking of the right thing to say. Only now I knew he was trying to think of the right lie.

"It's not that simple," he said. "That's naivety talking. Ask Jack about the many sides of right and wrong and all the shades of gray in the middle."

"I don't have to," I said, tilting my chin up with pride. "Jack stands on the side of what's right. *Always*."

"Maybe now, but ask him where the lines started to blur back when he was working on the fringe. Things get a little more complicated when you're wading your way through blood and money."

"Jack's a good man. Nothing you say will ever convince me otherwise."

Malachi nodded. "He is a good man. I couldn't have asked

for a better partner for my daughter or father for my future grandchildren. I wanted to see you and tell you congratulations. It was a beautiful wedding."

I didn't bother to ask how he knew that. It was obvious he'd been there in some capacity. It would have been even more thrilling to a man like Malachi to slip between the cracks with cops and FBI agents in the room. He was probably laughing all the way to the buffet table.

"You were here yesterday?" I asked. "When Jack and I came?"

He smiled and continued to jingle the change in his pocket. "I like places like this. It feels like having a home again, even if it's temporary. It's a good spot to keep up with what's going on in Bloody Mary. It's always refreshing to see that some things never change."

"Like what?" I asked.

"Sex, for one thing. This whole street is an episode of *Desperate Housewives*. Let me just say that this house gets a lot of activity for being vacant. That man across the street and the lady next door do things that you can only find on the internet. The realtor lady next door uses it as her personal boudoir and has entertained quite a few 'clients'. And her husband brings the cute little blonde from down the street here on her lunch hour since her husband sleeps during the day."

"What man across the street?" I asked. "How long have you been staying here?"

He shrugged. "Off and on for a while. It's a good house. It's furnished. And it has a crawl space in the attic that's easy to get to when people drop in unexpectedly. Which happens more often than you think."

"Who else?" I asked.

"Uh uh uh," he said. "My turn. You give some and you get some. That's how these things work."

"Oh, right," I said, smacking myself on the forehead. "For a second there I was under the illusion that you were just a father talking to his daughter."

"Sarcasm doesn't become you, Jaye."

"Sure it does," I said. "Ask anyone."

"Where are the missing flash drives?" he asked. "The ones from the boxes I had in the bunker."

"You mean the boxes you stole out of our safe?"

"They're my boxes. Technically, you stole them from me."

"Considering you're wanted by the FBI for a thousand heinous crimes, you don't really have claim to personal property anymore."

"You're not a child anymore, Jaye. It's time to grow up. Your mother and I were caught in the middle of a game that was bigger than just two people."

"That's what happens when you sell secrets to other countries," I explained patiently. "The people who originally hired you get mad and want to put you in prison."

"That's not what happened, and I can prove it. Those boxes are my salvation. They're your mother's salvation. We were soldiers. Just like so many others. We followed orders. And sometimes we were in so deep it was easy to forget we were the good guys. It was easy to forget what country we were fighting for. Governments are all the same. Don't let anyone ever tell you that one is better than the other. In the end, they'll all sacrifice you to save themselves."

Bitterness and anger shone briefly in his eyes before his face cleared of all expression. I could see the pulse pounding in the side of his neck. He wasn't as cool and collected as he wanted me to think.

"The things that are on those flash drives will put a lot of people in prison. Maybe I go down with them," he said, shrugging. "Who knows? But sometimes a house needs to be cleaned, and the best way to do that is to start at the top."

"I don't have them," I said. There was part of me that believed him. The other part of my brain was telling me how stupid I was for believing him.

His eyes narrowed. "You turned them over to someone," he said. "Someone with more tech skills than anyone in King George County. Son of a bitch," he said, turning and walking out of the room.

I was so surprised by his departure that I followed him. He was pacing back and forth across the floor, muttering to himself.

"Okay," he said. And then he took a deep breath and said, "Okay," again. "Logically, Jack would've turned to someone at the FBI. He's got friends there. But he also would want to keep it quiet. I've got tabs on the FBI database, and my name hasn't been flagged. Whoever's got them hasn't been able to crack my codes. I'm a hell of a lot better than any desk jockey they've got at the bureau nowadays."

I was pretty sure Ben Carver wouldn't be pleased to hear that.

"You've got to get them back for me, Jaye."

"What? No," I said, a little more forcefully that I'd planned. "I'm not helping you. You're a wanted man. A criminal. Helping you would make me a criminal too. I'm married to a cop. A cop who's running for re-election. Are you trying to screw up my life? Again?"

"Of course not," he said. "But this is bigger than us. I need help."

"There is no us," I said, shaking my head. "Just stop right there. I'm not helping you. In fact, I'm going to call Jack right now and let him know you're here. I've read the proof with my own eyes of the things you've done."

"You're read but a fraction of the story," he hissed. "You know nothing. I raised you better than this. To look at all the facts. To see things from every angle."

"You didn't raise me at all," I yelled, finally having enough. The tears had finally escaped, but I was too angry to care. "You tried raising another version of you. Someone who doesn't give a damn about anyone but themselves. Someone who circumvents channels when things don't go their way. Someone who cheats to get the outcome they want. Someone who will lie and steal and kill for ego and money. For the game."

"You think those lessons haven't served you well over the years?" he asked, his smile razor thin. "Tell me again how that cancer patient died when you were working at the hospital."

I felt the blood drain from my face.

"Maybe you're more my daughter than you want to give yourself credit for." He looked down at his watch. "Unfortunately, I have to go. Unless you've changed your mind about the flash drives."

I shook my head.

"Hardheaded," he said, as if I were the one in the wrong. "You know I'll get them eventually. With you or without you."

"It'll be without me," I said. "Let me make myself clear about that."

"In that case, we're going to have to part ways."

He took a step closer as if he were going to embrace me, and I froze. When was the last time he'd hugged me?

"It really was a beautiful wedding," he said, and then he used the side of his hand to chop at the pressure point at the side of my neck, and I was down for the count.

## 11

I FELT THE WOOLY TEXTURE OF THE RUG BENEATH MY FACE before I had the courage to try and open my eyes. When I did open them, the room spun as things came back into focus, so I closed them again.

I took in several deep breaths and waited for my stomach to settle before trying to focus. I had no idea how long I'd been out. It could've been seconds or hours. But either way, I had one hell of a headache.

I rolled onto my hands and knees and saw my phone a few feet away. I crawled toward it and checked the time, relieved to see it wasn't yet nine. I had twenty minutes to make the briefing at the station. If I was lucky, I'd keep my coffee down the whole way there. I needed to tell Jack what had happened, and I needed to tell him fast, before Malachi had a chance to go underground for good.

I left through the back door, not caring if anyone saw me leaving, and wobbled my way back toward the front of the house. Nothing had changed. Everyone was still going about the business. And there was still a killer on the loose.

The memory of Mrs. McGowen's murder made me want to kick myself. I'd taken one look at Malachi Graves and completely lost my senses. Why hadn't I asked him about Mrs. McGowen? Was it because I was afraid maybe *he* was the killer? There was certainly more than a chance he could be. And now that I knew he'd been living in the house, he'd have to be as high up on the person of interest list as Harrison Taylor.

I didn't notice the van parked in the driveway of Mrs. McGowen's house until I was almost back to the Suburban. I had to get a hold of myself. At what age would I stop letting my father rattle my cage?

The van was white and non-descript, but the side door was open and I could see a mountain of equipment and cleaning supplies.

"The sheriff gave me the all-clear," a soft, lilting voice said from behind me. It was about the most non-threatening voice I'd ever heard, but still, I jumped.

"Oh, Aoife," I said, putting a hand to my heart. "You snuck up on me."

Her look of confusion was understandable. She was standing plain as day in the middle of the driveway with a vacuum pack strapped to her back and a mop bucket in her hand.

Aoife Donovan, pronounced EE-fa, did crime-scene cleanup for the county. She barely came up to my shoulders and had a nice, soft look about her. Everything about her was soft. Her hair was a soft red. Her cheeks and body were softly rounded. She wasn't overweight, but she looked like the kind of woman who could give a comfortable hug. She had a smattering of freckles across the bridge of her nose and eyes the color of Irish moss. Her looks were the only soft thing about her. She didn't take crap from anybody. A high-profile divorce that left her pretty much destitute had toughened her up real fast.

She was dressed in a hazmat suit and had an oxygen mask hanging from her neck. Yellow industrial rubber gloves came up to her elbows and rubber fishing boots came up to her knees. She was dressed how I wish I'd been dressed the first time I'd gone into the house. Someone must've warned her. My guess was Jack. He had a soft spot for women who worked their tails off while trying to raise kids by themselves.

Aoife was a Bloody Mary transplant. She'd moved here from King George just after Christmas. She had a six-year-old son, a distrust of men, and a whole lot of gumption. She was about ten years older than me, and I adored her.

Jack's secretary, Betsy Clement, had decided to retire earlier than expected, so Jack had opened up the job search to replace her. In had walked Aoife, her son in tow because she couldn't afford to put him in daycare, and Jack had decided on the spot that whether or not she was the worst secretary on the face of the planet, she was going to be his.

Unfortunately, Betsy Clement was having a harder time retiring than she'd thought, which left Jack without a new secretary who wasn't a hundred years old, and Aoife without a job. And she'd really needed a job.

But she hadn't let the news get her down. She and Jack had put their heads together and made a list of all of Aoife's job skills. Since she'd been a housewife for the twelve years she'd been married, her talents mostly lent themselves to cookie baking and house cleaning. Which was when Jack came up with the idea of having an official crime scene clean up company. After Jack had gotten done spinning the position to the council and the community, you'd have thought it was the most needed position in the state.

Aoife said after changing diapers and being thrown up on, cleaning up crime scenes was kind of anti-climactic. It was statements like that one that made me glad I was still taking Lenny Kowalski's birth control pills. Kids were kind of gross.

"It's a mess in there," I said for lack of anything better.

She nodded soberly. "Reminds me of my granny's house. You couldn't swing a dick without hitting a cat. Half the time, I wasn't even sure if she knew what she was putting in the oven. Cats everywhere."

I was still caught on the swinging dick comment, so I didn't have a lot to offer as far as replies went.

"Well," I said, clearing my throat. "Good luck."

"As long as my check doesn't bounce I'll clean anything," she said. "This neighborhood is creepy as hell. It's like someone is always watching." Her eyes darted back and forth and I found myself looking up and down the street. It *was* creepy.

"Just for the record, I don't believe one word of what Madam Scandal wrote in her column."

"Thank you," I said, startled. "Honestly, I've forgotten all about it with the murder. Maybe everyone else has too."

"Doubtful," she said, matter-of-factly. "But maybe you and Jack should stay out of the back seats of vehicles."

My lips twitched. "Probably good advice."

"Not that I blame you. My ex used to have that kind of sex appeal. When we were first married, it was hard to keep my clothes on at all. It got easier though after most of the tri-state area became familiar with the birthmark shaped like Florida on his genitals."

I nodded in sympathy. Aoifa's husband had gotten caught with his pants down, literally, and had ended up being the focus of several unfortunate social media memes. I hated to tell her, but it was a heck of a lot more than the tri-state area that knew Paul Donovan's penis had paid homage to the sunshine state.

"Well, I've got to get to it," she said. "Those blood stains aren't going to clean themselves."

I waved goodbye and got in the Suburban, and then I drove the four blocks to the Town Square. The city complex was right in the middle of the square. The courthouse was on the left, the sheriff's office and jail in the middle, and the fire department was on the right. Parking was a nightmare no matter which building you were headed to.

I parked the Suburban in one of the spots reserved for city employees with a whole ten minutes left before the briefing started. I took a second to look in the rearview mirror and then quickly wished I hadn't. I looked like hell. My face was still pale and there were dark circles under my eyes. I could practically see the headache radiating across my skull. Jack was going to take one look at me and know something was terribly wrong.

I got out of the Suburban and locked the door before heading into the sheriff's office. From the outside, the city complex building looked beautiful. The architecture was Tudor, and it was a big white elephant of a building. In fact, the entire Town Square was Tudor, so it looked like a little English village. Which made sense, considering the names of the towns that made up King George County.

Where the outside was a white elephant, the inside was pure seventies revival. At least in the sheriff's office. I walked through the double glass doors into the entry area. It was a small operation, so there was a place to process those who'd been arrested in an area on the right, and on the left was where visitors could check in. One uniformed officer manned both desks. There was a Plexiglas partition and a locked door that separated the officers from the civilians.

"Hey, Riley," I said to the officer behind the desk. There was a young man in his early twenties handcuffed to the chair by the wall. He looked like he'd been greased from head to toe, and someone had worked him over pretty good. "Busy morning?"

"Not for me, Doc. But Lewis and Cole got called over to the Waffle Hut bright and early. It seems our friend and one of the waitresses have been having a Waffle Hut romance in the store room when it's not busy. Only this time the storeroom door didn't latch all the way and several angry customers came back to the kitchen to see what was taking their food so long. There was a scuffle, seeing how all those people weren't too keen on Billy here finishing up their breakfast."

"Understandable," I said. "Do I want to know why he looks like he just came through the birth canal?"

Riley chuckled. "Probably not, but I'll tell you anyway. It seems Crisco is Billy's lube of choice. The unfortunate part is that when Lewis and Cole arrived, Billy decided it was a good idea to run, but he was still mostly naked and a lot lubed up. That stuff doesn't just come off. So when Cole tackled him to the ground, it was more like wrestling a greased pig. Cole's been in the shower for twenty minutes. There's a pool going around to see if he's going to quit. Want in on it?"

"Nah, Cole won't quit. You know how much his mom likes to see him in uniform. He'd never disappoint her like that."

"Damn," Riley said. "I didn't think about that. I'm going to change my bet."

He hit the buzzer on the door and I walked through. The walls of the bullpen were painted mint green, and the flooring transitioned to gray tile. Pairs of wooden desks sat in uniformed rows, facing each other. There were five cells used for holding back to the right in a secured area, and Jack's office was to the left. It was a glass cube so he could see out and others could see in, but there were blinds on the windows that could be closed when privacy was needed.

I didn't see him in there, so I made my way to the conference room toward the back. The door was open, and I stuck my head in to make sure I was in the right place. Chen and Martinez leaned against the wall, talking quietly over their coffee. There was a large, square safe sitting at one end of the conference table and several boxes of things that had been collected at the scene.

"Morning, Doc," Martinez said. "Coffee is fresh."

"But is it good?" I asked.

"Sheriff made it," he said.

"In that case, I'll have some."

"He said he knows better than to not keep you caffeinated."

"One of the many reasons I married him," I said, pouring the black liquid into a Styrofoam cup.

"I'd love to hear the other reasons later," Jack said, walking in and closing the door behind him. "There are some days I wonder if you only keep me around for my coffee making skills."

"You're a good cook too," I said, making Chen and Martinez chuckle.

"You okay?" Jack asked, narrowing his eyes as he looked me over from head to toe.

"Eventful morning," I said, very aware of the others' curiosity.

He nodded and put a stack of files down on the table. "We're twenty-four hours into the investigation of Rosalyn McGowen's death. And so far, we have lots of questions and no answers. We have no murder weapon, and the only person on the street without an alibi is Harrison Taylor."

"Should we go ahead and start looking for other jobs?" Chen asked with a snort.

"Not just yet," Jack said. "I'll let you know after we talk to him." He filled Martinez and Chen in on what we'd discovered from the neighbors we'd talked to the day before. "Did you guys get any impressions on your end?" he asked.

"Monica Middleton," Chen said automatically. "She seemed nervous while we were talking to her. She works twelve hour shifts at the hospital, but she's off Friday through Sunday. I took it there was some estrangement between her and her husband. She said they were like ships passing in the night and they each kind of did their own thing. But it didn't seem like she wanted us to talk to him. He was asleep while we were there. He works nights and gets home about eight. He sleeps for a couple of hours and then gets up and goes to class."

"Katie Stein from across the street said she's seen a man there a couple of times in the middle of the night," Jack said. "She thinks she's having an affair."

After speaking with my father, I knew this information to be true, but I couldn't say anything until I'd had a chance to talk to Jack.

"That would explain the nervousness," Martinez said. "She kept looking toward the bedroom. But everyone else on the street seemed like normal families. They go to work. They have a consistent routine. Everyone adored Mrs. McGowen."

"What about Abby Clearwater?" Jack asked.

Chen let out a laugh and cut her eyes to Martinez. It was impossible to miss the slight pink tinge to Martinez's cheeks.

"You mean the hot blonde who answered the door wearing the tiniest shorts I've ever seen in my life and a tank top without a bra? That Abby Clearwater?" Chen slapped Martinez on the back. "He was a puddle at her feet. She was so distraught you'd have thought she'd found the body herself, and Casanova here did everything from bringing her water to offering to make her homemade soup."

"It was the nice thing to do," Martinez said. "My mama taught me to take care of women when they're upset."

"Yeah, she was so upset her hand almost got stuck slipping her number in your back pocket."

Martinez grinned, showing the dimple in his cheek. "Sometimes you've gotta make house calls. Isn't that right, Doc?"

"Oh, I'm getting nowhere near this one," I said. "What you do on your house calls is your own business."

"Maybe wait to sleep with her until after we clear her of murder," Jack said. "It would look bad for the department."

"You got it, Sheriff. But seriously, I'd move next door in a heartbeat. It was like a sign from God seeing that For Sale sign."

"That house is way out of your price range, Martinez," Jack said.

"Maybe the cat lady's house will be cheaper. I have to assume it'll go on the market soon. No one likes to live in a house where someone was murdered."

"Men are so weird," Chen said. "You're making life plans based on the fact that you met a woman one time. One. Time."

"What can I say? I'm a romantic."

"Did Abby's story mesh with Robert and Janet?" I asked.

"Sure did," Martinez said. "She said they left the house right at five-thirty and then everyone grouped off in their normal groups. She's said she's always very aware of where Harrison is because he cornered her one time and she didn't think she was going to get out of that situation without someone getting hurt. But she's training for a half-marathon, so she's needing the extra miles. She runs six days a week. She said she ran with Robert and Janet for about a mile or so and she split off from them when she figured Harrison was far enough in the other direction. She ran another ten miles, so she didn't get back home for another couple of hours."

"Can anyone confirm?" Jack asked.

"She says she didn't see anyone, but she showed us her route. My gut says she's on the up and up," Martinez said.

"Your gut kept staring at her tits," Chen said. "I don't think your gut is qualified."

"See if you can find anyone to corroborate," Jack said. "If either of y'all are interested, we've got access to Rosalyn McGowen's financials and last will and testament."

"Who are her beneficiaries?" I asked.

"She has no living family, so her beneficiaries are pretty varied. Lots of charities and foundations. It's her bank accounts that are interesting. She made a killing of the sale of her bakery several years ago. We're talking multi-millions. But she's got steady income coming in from somewhere else. Money is being directly deposited into one of her accounts at random intervals. It's never the same amounts and it's never the same time. Sometimes she gets deposits every day."

"How much money?" Martinez asked.

"I haven't had time to go back farther than a couple of months, but it already totals more than a million dollars."

Martinez whistled. "She was a rich old lady. Makes you wonder who knew it?"

"She never touched the money," Jack continued. "Only deposits were being made into that account. No withdrawals. She lived frugally off the money she'd received from the sale of the bakery. Her house had long since been paid for, and her car was paid for. Her only expenses were small monthly bills. She tithed consistently to St. Paul's every month, and she was a member of a weekly delivery service for pets. I guess someone came to change out cat litter and deliver bags of food. The majority of her expenses went to the grocery store. She spent enough every week to feed a family of ten."

"That makes sense," I said. "She was baking for the whole neighborhood and anyone else she passed by. Her having that kind of money already makes it seem less likely someone would be after something as simple as recipes from that laptop."

"That was my thinking too," Jack said. "Maybe they thought they could get into her accounts if they got the laptop. But there's no sign of money being moved around."

"Maybe they didn't take her laptop at all. Maybe it's been in the safe the whole time."

"I'm waiting for the safe company to call me back with the override code. They received the electronic warrant this morning."

Jack's cell phone rang seconds later. The conversation was short and to the point, and Jack wrote down a series of numbers on his notepad. He thanked whoever was on the other line and hung up.

"Let's see what all the fuss is about," he said.

"I can understand why she'd have a safe with those security measures with the kind of cash she has," I said.

"There's got to be something more to this," Martinez insisted. "A million bucks worth of deposits over two months period of time doesn't exactly say uninvolved old lady. She was clearly involved in something. And we didn't get any reports of her selling her baked goods. Which means she was selling something else."

"Edna Bright said she thought Mrs. McGowen was a madam because of the unusual hours she kept, coming and going in the middle of the night. It's just hard to believe the Mrs. McGowen we knew could be someone with such a dark secret."

"We knew the woman who gave us cookies and lemonade after school," Jack said. "But we didn't *know* her. Money is a powerful motivator for a lot of people. And it's more than likely the reason she's dead."

Jack went to the safe and typed in the override code, and I held my breath as I heard the lock click and the pressurized door open. I wasn't sure what I was expecting to see inside the safe. We had a safe at home and we kept cash and our personal papers inside of it. We didn't keep as much cash as Rosalyn McGowen kept in hers though.

"Holy shit," Martinez said.

"I did a bust once in Atlanta on a drug dealer that had this much cash in his safe," Chen said. "It's the only time I've ever seen anything like it."

Jack put on a pair of gloves and said, "If you'll record, Martinez." And then he pulled out the stacks of bills, neatly bound with a paper wrapping and started counting.

"A hundred thousand even," Jack said.

I wasn't as interested in the money he'd pulled out of the safe as I was in the fact that I couldn't see a laptop. There was a high quality digital camera and a place where it was obvious a laptop would fit.

"I was hoping it would be easy," Jack said.

"What about the beneficiaries?" I asked.

"There's no big bulk that goes to any one individual. Don't get me wrong, she's left nice chunks of change to different organizations, but nothing that seems suspicious at first glance." He opened one of the files and read down the list. "She left money to the American Heart Association, the Culinary Institute, the King George Historical Society, the King George Cemetery Association, the Bloody Mary Architects, LLC…"

"The Bloody Mary Architects?" I asked. "What the hell organization is that?"

"Quarter," three people echoed back at me.

I said a whole bunch of swear words in my head. Whose stupid idea was the quarter jar anyway? "Hell is a place, not a swear word."

"I've never heard of The Bloody Mary Architects," Jack said. "We'll have to do a little digging. She's also left small amounts to various businesses in town, those that are small and owned by friends of hers."

"What about the house?" I asked, thinking of how bad Janet Selby wanted to get her hooks into it.

Jack flipped through several pages, reading quickly, and then raised his brows. "She left the house to Carl Planter. She says because she knows he'll do the best job fixing it up for another couple to enjoy as much as she and her husband enjoyed it."

"Well, that's something," I said. "And he was the last person to see her alive."

"We'll pay him another visit," Jack said. "It's enough to get a warrant to look into his finances. Maybe the construction business isn't doing so well."

Jack took the camera out next and handed it over to Martinez. "Why don't you and Chen see what you can find on here? It might be nothing but cats, but we need to look."

"It hooks up directly to the computer," Chen said. "She'd more than likely download everything onto her laptop."

"You said you didn't find a phone either?" I asked.

"We found a charger in her car and one plugged in next to her bed. But no phones."

"Then she's got her phone and computer linked. Whoever

took them either wanted what was on them, or they didn't want anyone else to see what was on them."

"Blackmail?" Jack asked, narrowing his eyes in thought. "That would be an interesting twist on things. And it could explain the deposits."

"That's a hell of a lot of blackmail," Martinez said.

"You guys start digging deeper on everyone in the neighborhood and see what you can find with the camera," Jack said. "I'll get started on the warrant for Carl's financials and then we'll go have another chat with him. And I'll call in some extra help to see if we can figure out where those deposits are coming from."

There was only one person Jack called in for work like that. Jack and Ben Carver had been friends for years, but Ben owed Jack his life and he was always willing to use his skills and position in the FBI to help where help was needed. Jack trusted Ben with his life, which was why he was also the man we'd given Malachi's flash drives to.

The thought of Ben had me thinking about my dad and my run-in with him earlier. It seemed like a lifetime ago instead of an hour.

"You got it, Sheriff," Chen said.

"We're going on the next twenty-four hours without a lot to show for it," Jack said. "Let's start putting some pressure on people."

# 12

Jack got a call before I could get a chance to fill him in on my dad, so I made my way toward his office. It was barely ten o'clock, and my thoughts were consumed with my dad. If I'd been paying attention, I would've felt someone moving in behind me. As it was, I was completely caught off guard.

"Damn, Jaye," a man said, slipping an arm around me in what probably looked like a casual hug to anyone looking through the glass windows. But a hand squeezed my breast and I pushed out of his grasp. "Married life suits you. You're looking good. Or maybe it's just that you're forbidden fruit."

I was struck dumb for a few seconds, my brain trying to comprehend the action, the words, and who the hell had touched me. Harrison Taylor stood beaming at me, his pose casual and a hand in his pocket, now that I'd put some distance between us.

He was a handsome man—classically handsome—there

was no disputing that. His face was angular and his features even. His dark blond hair was thick and perfectly cut and combed, and his teeth were blindingly white. The suit he wore was lightweight and charcoal in color, and his tie was red and silver striped. But despite his attractiveness, there was a knowing smirk in his eyes that told me he'd known exactly what he'd done. And more than likely, it was a common practice.

"I don't like to be hugged," I said, my voice cold enough to make ice cubes.

"Hmm," he said. "Maybe that's why your husband is seeking attention in the back of his cruiser instead of in his marriage bed. Sometimes a woman just needs the right teacher."

"And sometimes a woman is happily married and sees easily through the slime."

He smiled liked we were making small talk about the good old days. Anyone walking by the office would've thought just that.

"You always did have teeth, Jaye. I like that about you. It makes for a feisty opponent."

"There's no game here for us to be on opposing sides. And you want to watch your step. I won't be intimidated like your law clerks and secretaries that put up with your bull-shit because they need to keep their jobs."

His smile dimmed a notch, but he kept it in place. "You're going to want to be careful. You don't want to be on my bad side."

"That's funny," I said, "because I was just going to tell you the same thing."

I saw Jack walking in front of the windows and let out a breath of relief. There wasn't a shred of doubt in my mind that Harrison Taylor could've killed Mrs. McGowen.

"Harrison," Jack said, coming into the office. He took one look at me and knew something had happened, but he went through the pleasantries anyway. Politics was a bitch, and there was a time and place for everything when you lived in the public eye. "I was just coming to find you. We spoke to your wife yesterday."

"Yes, she mentioned you came by. It's a shame about Rosie. Everyone loved her."

Jack stood behind his desk, but didn't offer Harrison a seat. I doubted he would've taken it if it had been offered. He wouldn't want the subordinate position.

"You're a member of the running club?" Jack asked.

"I'm sure you already know that," Harrison said. "Everyone on that street knows more than they should about everyone else and loves to talk to whoever will listen. It's one of the reasons I prefer to run ahead of the group. If they spent more time focused on running instead of chatting, they'd all be in a lot better shape."

"Did you take off at the same time as the rest of the group on Monday?"

"I did," he said, shrugging. "Just like always."

"Did you notice any activity at Rosalyn McGowen's place?"

"Everything was just like normal. Her windows were open, and we could all smell something baking. Her lights were on. Since it was five-thirty in the morning, her house was lit up like a Christmas tree compared to the rest of the block."

"What about when you returned home after the run?"

He frowned and studied Jack. "I don't know," he said. "I honestly wasn't paying much attention. I was focused on getting back and getting to the office. I had court that morning." He picked a piece of lint off his sleeve and smiled again. "You know, people make mistakes all the time. Maybe you're looking for a murder investigation where there isn't one. Those kinds of headlines are great during an election season. Maybe it's just another tragedy that's befallen an elder living alone."

"That would be easy to believe except for the fact that someone bashed her over the head," I said. "You said it yourself. Everyone in that neighborhood knows more than they should and they like to talk about it. I wonder what it was that Mrs. McGowen knew that got her killed."

His smile tightened, but stayed in place. I had to give him credit where credit was due. Harrison Taylor wasn't a man who lost control easily. He was cold and ruthless.

"It's anyone's guess. Sorry, Jack, but I've got to cut this short. I have appointments to keep. You're a lucky man. Congratulations on your marriage." He turned to me. "Jaye…" he said, the smirk coming back into his eyes. "I'm sure we'll run into each other again."

I resisted the urge to yell out, "over my dead body," and instead watched him turn on his heel and walk away.

"You okay?" Jack asked for the second time that morning.

"Yes, but if I ever end up in a room alone again with Harrison Taylor, he's probably going to end up with a broken face. No wonder the women on that street surround themselves with protection. He doesn't like to take no for an answer."

"Do I need to kill him?"

"Not yet," I said. "But I'll let you know."

"Harrison could've killed her," Jack said. "He's got the temperament."

"Oh, yeah," I said, blowing out a breath.

"I put in the request for a warrant to Judge Reiner for Carl Planter's financials. We need to go talk to Richard Selby. He's back from his conference and working at the clinic today. And then we need to talk to Maria Clark." He put his hand on the back of my neck and massaged the tension there. "And maybe on the way, you could tell me why you were so upset when you came in this morning."

---

I WAITED until Jack had gotten away from the square and we were on our way to the King George Veterinary Clinic. It was out a ways, in a rural area, because it had a barn attached for some of the larger animals and sometimes they had to stay for extended periods of time while they were on the mend.

"You remember how I thought someone was in that vacant house yesterday?" I asked.

"I do," he said, stopping at a red light.

"It turns out I was right. I ran into my father this morning."

"I'm assuming there's a good reason you didn't call me immediately to come pick him up."

I could hear the tight accusation in Jack's tone, and I really wasn't in the mood for it after the morning I'd had.

"Yeah," I said, the tone of my voice full of attitude. "It was probably the fact that I was passed out on the floor after he chopped me in the neck. When I woke up he was gone. Otherwise, I would've called you right away. Promise." My last words were saccharine sweet and I saw Jack wince.

"Sorry," he said, blowing out a breath. "I know you would've called if you could've."

"Believe me, Jack. I know the kind of man my father is better than you. I'm the last person who would try to protect him after everything he's done."

"I know that too. I'm sorry," he said again. "How did you find him? Or how did he find you?"

"I had some time to kill this morning before the meeting, so I wanted to drive the streets behind each side of Foxglove Court. I started thinking about the trek through the woods in the middle of the night and that the easiest way to accomplish the goal was to already be established in the neighborhood. It would just be a huge pain in the ass to park, walk through the woods in the dark, scale a creek with a twenty-foot drop, and not be dog tired by the time you got to her house to kill her. And if you say *quarter* to me right now I'm going to lose my religion."

Jack's lips twitched. "I wouldn't think of it. Keep going."

"I parked in front of the crime scene and then walked across the street to the vacant house. I tried the front door and it was locked, but when I went around to the back, the door was open. I'd still swear the house was empty when I went in. You know how you can feel when you're not alone? I walked through the house and never had a sense that there was anyone else there but me. But when I went to the front bedroom where I saw the curtain move, he was there when I turned around to leave."

"Let me guess," he said. "He wants the flash drives."

"Right in one," I said. "Well, he wanted the flash drives and to let me know that he enjoyed our wedding."

"Son of a bitch," Jack said, lightly hitting his hand on the steering wheel. "Of course he'd want to be there, moving in and out of all those cops. It was probably the biggest high of his life."

"I said pretty much the same thing. He also said those flash drives are his salvation. That whatever information that's on there is enough to exonerate him and my mother, and to bring everyone at the top of different government agencies to the ground. He asked for my help."

"What did you tell him?"

"That I was going to call you so you could arrest him. That's when he incapacitated me. I wasn't out for very long. Maybe a few minutes. But when I woke up, he was long gone. I didn't see a car or any kind of transportation nearby, so I don't know where he went or how he got there in the first place.

"He also told me that the vacant house was getting a lot of action. Apparently, the neighborhood was taking advantage of it for their liaisons. He said Richard Selby is the one having the affair with Monica. And he also said the man across the street was having an affair with the woman next door. You don't think he meant Robert or Carl, do you?"

"Who knows," Jack said. "Stranger things have happened. Katie said she saw the mystery man in Monica's house just before midnight on Sunday. If it was Richard, that means he wasn't in DC for the conference after all."

"I guess we need to ask him then."

# 13

THE VET CLINIC WAS NOT THE MOST CONVENIENT PLACE TO get to, but it served all four towns, though there was a smaller clinic on the south side of the county.

The clinic itself was a tan metal building that sat on a patch of green field. The parking lot was gravel, and there was a big red metal barn attached to the back side of the clinic. There was a fenced in area where two horses grazed lazily. The parking lot was full of cars, and there was a horse trailer pulled along the side of the building.

Jack parked his unit toward the back of the lot, and our shoes crunched the gravel as we walked toward the building. He opened the door and a bell jingled from above. A blast of cool air and the distinct smell of animals and disinfectant greeted us.

We walked into a waiting room of chaos. Dogs and cats sat with their owners. There were barks and hisses and meows, and a harried looking receptionist sat behind the desk with a phone to her ear. She was petite with bright red hair cut like a pixie's, and she wore black framed glasses on a chain around her neck. She was writing frantically in her appointment book and chewing gum a mile a minute.

When she hung up, she spotted us and a look of defeat came over her face. "Dr. Selby really doesn't have time to talk to you right now," she said apologetically, obviously recognizing us and knowing why we were there. "He's been gone all week and the waiting room is backed up."

"We wouldn't do it if it weren't absolutely necessary," Jack said. "We'll try to be as quick as we can, but human life is our priority."

"Don't let some of these people hear you say that," she whispered. "There will be a riot. Y'all can follow me back and I'll get the doctor."

We went through a wood-paneled door into a long hallway that smelled like antiseptic and dog shampoo. Richard Selby's diplomas hung on the wall. There were a couple of treatment rooms to the right and an area where they weighed and measured the animals to the left. The receptionist led us into a room that was something of a catch-all. There was a mini-fridge and a long counter with various supplies. A shelf with packaged syringes of various sizes sat on the counter. There were unopened boxes pushed against one wall and a huge industrial sized bathtub in the back, raised about three feet off the ground.

She left us in there to wait and I tried to get a closer look at the samples of medicines and other vials left out in the open. There were no narcotics. Just locals and mild sedatives.

"Sheriff," Richard Selby said as he came in. He pulled off

his gloves and tossed them in the trash before reaching out to shake Jack's hand, and then mine. His smile was friendly, even though he looked distracted. "You caught me on a tight schedule today."

"We'll be quick," Jack assured him. "I'm sure you've heard Rosalyn McGowen was murdered early Monday morning."

"Yes, it's terrible. She was the sweetest woman. Always doing for someone. She reminded me of my grandma. When the kids were born, she set us up with meals for a week and knitted blankets for each of the kids."

I was having a hard time putting Richard and Janet Selby together as a couple. The talkative, critical woman we'd met the day before didn't seem to go with the man we were meeting today. Janet had shown a lot of resentment when she spoke of her husband, which made me think she knew about his affair.

"Janet called as soon as she heard the news. I actually came back from my conference early last night. I'd originally planned to drive back from DC this morning and open the clinic late, but after I saw the backlog of appointments I decided it was best to bite the bullet and head home early. Plus, it sounded like Janet was taking the news of Roz's death pretty hard when I talked to her."

"What time did you leave on Sunday for your conference?" Jack asked.

"About noon," he said. "It took me close to two hours with the traffic, and I had a drink in the bar once I got to the hotel with a couple of friends. They opened up for check-in about three."

"What can you tell us about your relationship with Monica Middleton?"

I saw it. It was just a flash of fear, but it was there in his eyes before he smiled again. "Sure, I know Monica. She and her husband live on the street. We're all pretty close on Foxglove Court."

"Do you have a sexual relationship with her?"

"No, of course not," he said. "I'm a happily married man. I've got a business. The Selbys are sixth generation in Bloody Mary."

"A neighbor told us they saw you through the window at Monica's around midnight on Monday night. And we had another report that you and Monica frequently use the vacant house next to yours to meet up."

Richard seemed to deflate in front of our eyes and he leaned back against the counter. He put his head in his hand and rubbed at his brow.

"Does Janet know?" he asked.

"I don't know the answer to that," Jack said. "But in my experience, they always know. They just might not want to face the truth. My job here is to find a murderer. That's all."

Richard blew out a long breath. "It's times like this when I wish I'd never quit smoking. This is tobacco country, and all you see everywhere is warnings on how the things will kill you. I never really cared much that they're bad for you. But then you have kids and it's hard to explain to them why you'd keep doing something that's bad for you.

"That's kind of how I feel about Monica. I know it's not

going anywhere. We're both married. We're both entrenched in our own lives and own circles. It was just one of those things," he said, shrugging. He was looking off in the distance as if we weren't even there. "I knew it was wrong, and I swear to God it's never happened before. But I found myself working harder and longer hours here, and when I'd get home, Janet would already be drinking. And Lord, that woman never shuts up. She never hears a word I say or listens to what I want.

"And then last summer we were having our monthly barbecue at the Miller's house. Everyone is in bathing suits and drinking and having a good time. I'd gone in to grab a beer out of the fridge and she was sitting on one of the barstools looking out at everyone having fun. Her husband hadn't come to the barbecue, and she just looked…sad.

"We started talking and before we knew it, we'd made plans to have coffee one morning before we both left for work. The timing worked out perfectly when the Goldmans won the lottery and the house went up for sale. It wasn't hard to get a copy of the key to the house next door. Janet's one of those people who doesn't get out of bed before nine, so I didn't worry about her noticing what was going on at seven in the morning. It started out innocently. I'd bring the coffee and we'd sit and talk until it was time to leave. But there was a connection there. We both felt it. And it wasn't long before I'd wait for Janet and the kids to go to sleep and I'd slip down to Monica's house for a few hours. It was like a drug. I wanted to be with her. She listened to me and I could share anything with her.

"And then it stopped being so innocent." He stopped and smiled like he'd been lost in the memory. "She met me at her back door one night wearing absolutely nothing. I don't know how long I stood at the threshold of that door wondering what choice I would make. Ultimately, I walked over the threshold, and I've felt guilty about it every day since."

"But you didn't stop," I said matter-of-factly.

There was part of me that felt sympathy for Richard Selby. But as someone who'd had the experience of being cheated on, I had very little tolerance for cheaters or their excuses. It's what they chose to do after the fact that showed their character. Janet Selby clearly had problems and had contributed to the issues in their marriage, but marriage was a two-way street, and she didn't deserve what he was doing to her.

He sighed and said, "No, I didn't stop. Not until Monday night when I went to see Monica for the last time. The affair cooled off a few months ago, but it had become more of a habit than a need. I knew for Janet and I to have any chance at fixing whatever is left of our marriage, I had to put a stop to that part of things. I'd planned to tell Janet what I'd done. But I guess this makes it more of a reality. Especially if the neighbors know. I don't want her to hear it from someone besides me." He broke down, a sob catching in his throat and he buried his face in his hands. "I'm afraid she's going to leave me."

I glanced at Jack and saw he was as at a loss for words as I was. This wasn't where we'd seen the conversation going.

"Dr. Selby," Jack said softly. "For what it's worth, I think you're doing the right thing. But I need to ask what you did after you left Monica's. And can anyone confirm your whereabouts?"

"I left," he said, grabbing a paper towel from the holder on the wall and wiping his face. "I parked a couple of streets over, so I just walked back to the car and drove back to the hotel. I had a seven-thirty tee time the next morning. I guess the hotel cameras would have me coming back."

"We'll check it out," Jack said. "We appreciate your time."

Richard didn't tell us goodbye. He seemed shell-shocked, and he was just staring off into space when we left.

---

WHEN WE GOT BACK in the car, the electronic warrant for Carl's financials had come through, and Jack put in a call to Martinez to send him the information once he got it. Then he put in another call, and I felt my body tense as I realized who was on the other line.

"Carver," Jack said, putting him on speaker phone. "What are your weekend plans?"

Ben Carver was one of my favorite people, but he was the last person I wanted Jack to call at the moment. My dad would go to any lengths to get those flash drives back, and Ben was currently in possession of them. If it came down to my dad's life or an FBI agent he didn't know, I could guess which he'd choose.

"It's funny you should ask," Carver said. "Someone gave my wife a weekend at a spa as one of her baby shower gifts. She packed a bag and left this morning. It took me twenty minutes to find the baby. She likes to hide. And someone put peanut butter on my electric shaver. I don't know who gave Michelle that gift card, but I'm going to hunt them down and kill them. She packed a lot of clothes. I'm not sure she's coming back. She sent me a text that said she'd send me a picture of the baby once she's born."

I laughed and wiped tears from my eyes. Ben was high energy. If I had to guess, I'd say his wife was escaping from him as much as the kids. I'd never had the opportunity to meet his wife, but she sounded like an incredible woman. She had a PhD in English and she'd given birth the three girls in the last three years and was pregnant with their fourth.

"Why?" Ben asked. "What have you got going on?"

"I was going to see if you wanted to visit for the weekend and bring Miranda," Jack said. "But since you're on dad duty…"

"Are you kidding me? If duty calls, Miranda and I will be there. You'll tell Michelle it's for work won't you? She probably won't believe me."

Jack's lips twitched and he said, "I'll write you a note."

"Let me call my mother-in-law," Ben interrupted. "She's been calling every half hour since Michelle left. She's afraid something will go wrong. I haven't told her about losing Sophie so I'd appreciate it if you'd keep that to yourself."

"Your secret is safe with me," Jack said. "Bring the flash drives."

"Will do," Ben said. "But I told you I haven't been able to encrypt them. Whoever put the security on those things is a freaking genius. If I do it wrong, the whole thing will be destroyed."

"We'll deal with that when the time comes."

"I can be there about dinner time," Ben said.

Jack laughed. "Of course you can," he said and hung up.

We drove past the Town Square to Main Street, and then took a right onto Purgatory. It was actually a pretty cool street with boutique shops and a café. Jack parked in front of *Sole Mates* and we got out to talk to Maria Green.

The BOGO sign was out on the sidewalk, but sidewalk traffic was light, and there was no one in the store. Maria stood in front of a display case, taking shoes out of boxes and putting the display shoes on the shelf.

She was a pretty woman. Young. Hispanic. Probably mid-twenties and voluptuous. Her pregnancy was just starting to show. Her hair was long and dark, and a fringe of bangs framed exotic black eyes. Her red dress hugged her body and emphasized the slight curve of her belly and an impressive showing of cleavage. She stood on four-inch stilettos. If there was anyone ever to exude sex appeal, it was Maria Green.

"Good morning," she said, smiling at us over her shoulder. "Everything is buy one, get one half off." Her accent was thick.

"I'm Sheriff Lawson, and this is Doctor Graves," he said, showing her his badge. "We're here to talk to you about Rosalyn McGowen."

Her expression fell, and I saw genuine sadness in her eyes.

"Such a sweet woman. But I already talked to the police officers yesterday. I didn't see anything." She put down the shoes and came over to us. "The baby makes me so sleepy. It's a good thing the store doesn't open until ten. I would never make it. I go to bed and sleep like the dead, and when I wake up I'm sick as a dog. Everyone tells me it will pass."

She said the words, but she didn't look like she believed them.

"I'm here to see if you can fill in some details," Jack said. "Why don't we sit down since you don't have any customers at the moment?"

The store wasn't very big, but there was a large ottoman in the middle of the floor that could seat at least six people, and there were two ladies' chairs angled next to the floor to ceiling mirror. Maria and I took the chairs, and Jack sat across from us on the ottoman.

"This might seem like an odd thing to ask, but Mrs. McGowen's murder is very unusual. We believe whoever killed her was very familiar with her schedule. Not only her schedule, but they're familiar enough with everyone on the street's schedule that they could slip in and out without anyone seeing them."

Maria cocked her head and stared blankly at us for a few seconds, and then raised her brows in surprise. "You think someone on Foxglove Court killed her?" She brought her hand to her stomach in a protective gesture. "One of my neighbors is a murderer?"

"We think so, yes," Jack said. "And you might want to keep that bit of information to yourself for the time being."

She waved away the suggestion. "No one talks to me much," she said matter-of-factly. "No one but Katie and Rosie. And Robert and Carl are very nice, but they are always gone. I don't think I fit in. Someone has called immigration on me twice. I'm an American citizen," she said passionately, her chin going up a notch.

"Who do you think did that?" Jack asked.

"I think it's that no good Harrison Taylor. Or maybe his wife. I have a way of making an impression on men," she said, a satisfied smile crossing her face. "I am from Colombia. When a married man touches you in ways you have not invited, you grab him by the balls and squeeze until they cry like little girls." She made a closed fist like she was squeezing his balls, and I wished I could've witnessed that event. "Now when he sees me, he scowls and runs away like the rat he is."

"What was he like toward Mrs. McGowen?" Jack asked.

"He hated those cats," she said, shaking her head. "One of them gets out from time to time. Harrison came out one morning and the cat was on the hood of his car. I could hear him yelling all the way down the street. Everyone came outside to see what the fuss was about. Harrison said he was getting his gun and was going to shoot the cat, so Carl went over and got it off the hood and took it back to Rosie."

"Have there been any other incidents like that?"

"Not really," she said, shrugging. "It's quiet for the most part. Everyone watches out for each other. It's nice to be able to go away for a weekend and have someone watch the house or water the plants. Those kinds of things. It's just impossible to think that something like what happened to Rosie happened on our street."

"What about Richard Selby?"

She hesitated and broke eye contact, thinking it through before she answered. "He's very quiet. Seems to work a lot. But he has kind eyes. I don't think his marriage is a happy one."

"What about Monica Middleton?"

She let out a breath. "Then you know?"

"About their relationship?" Jack asked. "Yes, we know."

"I saw him sneaking through the trees one night. Just his shadow at first, but he came into the light enough that I saw his face. We have a big spotlight in the back because it gets so dark and Clark is always worried about intruders. I tell him this isn't the kind of place like that, but we lived in Miami for several years before coming here, and old habits are hard to break."

"No one else besides Harrison had any problems with Rosalyn?" Jack asked.

"No," she said, shaking her head. "Not that I know of. She was just a nice old lady."

# 14

A LONG TIME HAD PASSED SINCE BREAKFAST, AND I NEEDED to put something in my stomach and then head to the funeral home.

"What do you want for lunch?" Jack asked.

"I don't care. What do you feel like?"

I knew from experience that the subject of where to eat was a vicious cycle and one of the most difficult questions to answer in marriage.

"I feel like a burrito," Jack said.

"Go to *Nacho Taco*. There's a burger place right next door and we can go to both."

"Why didn't you just say you wanted a burger?" he asked, turning to look at me. "Why can't we just go to one place?"

"Because I want you to be happy and get what you want to eat. This way, we both get what we want."

"That makes no sense," he said.

I was pretty sure he was going to expound on that, but a call came in on his radio. Kendra Cormac was the daytime dispatcher for the county.

"Sheriff, a call came in a few minutes ago of a reported gunshot at 409 Foxglove Court. I know that's Rosalyn McGowen's street and figured you'd want to check it out yourself."

"Thanks, Kendra. Heading that direction now."

"Gunshot," I said. "Who lives at 409?"

"Carl and Robert."

Jack turned on his lights and sirens and thoughts of lunch were forgotten. We turned onto Foxglove Court a few minutes later. I recognized all but a couple of the faces standing in Robert and Carl's yard, but I knew by process of elimination that one was Keith Middleton, Monica's husband, and the couple standing arm in arm had to be Tom and Lynette Miller.

Janet Selby was there, her arms around two boys in their early teenage years. She was wearing yoga pants and a long sleeve Lycra shirt, and her hair was up in a ponytail and sweaty at the temples.

Frank and Edna Bright were on their front porch, watching from afar and not interacting with the others. Abby Clearwater stood just behind Janet, holding the hand of Katie's soap opera obsessed toddler. Katie sat on the front porch, Robert's head against her bosom and her arms around his shaking, sobbing body.

Everyone had a shell-shocked, deer in the headlights look about them as they stood and watched. Robert's blue Prius was in the driveway, the trunk open and bags of groceries still in the back. Carl's truck was also in the driveway, which didn't jibe with what he'd said about getting home from work every day around four o'clock.

Jack left his lights on, but turned off the sirens, and we got out of the car and headed to the porch. Katie looked up at us with tear drenched eyes and shook her head, like she wasn't quite sure what to say.

"Robert," Jack said softly, kneeling next to them on the porch stairs. "Can you tell me what happened?"

Robert kept sobbing as if Jack's words hadn't penetrated at all. I'd seen grief like this often enough to know that he probably hadn't heard. Jack looked up to Katie.

"Someone called 911 when a gunshot was heard," he said.

She nodded and kept stroking Robert's back like he was a child. "Inside," she whispered. "Carl's inside."

"Robert, I'm going inside now," Jack said. "I'm going to see Carl."

I'd grabbed a pair of gloves out of habit, and I opened the screen door, holding it open for Jack.

There was a smell about death. And new death smelled different than old death. Old death hinted of dust and decay. But with new death came the coppery tang of blood and the release of bladder and bowels that tended to coat the inside of the nostrils and throat. It was a smell you got used to if you were around it enough.

"Damn," Jack said. There wasn't a body in sight, but we knew there would be one.

The house looked the same as it had the day before—bright and light and cheerful. I noticed the grocery bags just like the ones in the trunk of the Prius on the kitchen counter. One of them had fallen off and bright yellow lemons had rolled across the floor.

We hadn't gone into the other parts of the house the day before, so we were unfamiliar with the layout, but it didn't take long to find Carl Planter. He was in the hall bathroom, fully clothed in the bathtub, a revolver on the floor just below his limp hand.

"I'll get my bag," I said and headed back to the car. It wasn't often that we arrived at scenes that fresh. Pristine was another question. Usually whoever found the victim touched the body, checking to see if they were still alive, contaminating the scene in some way. Suicides were all worked as homicides until the suicide could be determined for sure.

I suited up at the car and pulled my hair back. That seemed to set off a reaction from the onlookers and several of them started crying. I texted Sheldon and let him know he needed to bring the Suburban for a pick up and gave him the address. Lily and Tyler were both in class for most of the day, and they'd be upset they'd missed the autopsy opportunity, but I couldn't wait on them.

Robert and Katie hadn't moved from the front steps, though Robert's sobs had subsided some. Neither of them paid attention to me as I moved around them and headed back inside. Jack stood in the hallway outside of the bathroom, and I handed him a pair of gloves.

"I've called it in," he said. "I need to talk to Robert. The sooner the better."

"You find a note?" I asked.

"Not yet, but I haven't looked anywhere but the bathroom."

"It's convenient he did it in the tub," I said. "Makes the cleanup easier."

"Carl seemed like a pretty thoughtful guy," Jack said, but it was something to put away for later.

The bathroom was directly across from the guest bedroom, and I assumed that was its intended purpose. I found it odd that Carl would choose the guest bath to take his life in. Usually people wanted the comfort of the familiar before they ended things.

The bathroom had a modernized fifties feel to it with a white pedestal sink and a claw foot tub. The walls were mint green on the top half and white wainscoting on the bottom half. There were built-in shelves above the toilet with neatly stacked white towels in various sizes and candle artfully arranged. The shower rod hung from the ceiling and was in the shape of an oval, so the curtain could be pulled all the way around the freestanding tub.

I hated to see Carl this way. I'd enjoyed our conversation the day before, and I'd instantly liked him and Robert. Seeing him now was a very different picture from the vibrant man I'd met the day before.

Carl was a big man, and he took up every inch of the tiny claw foot, his legs bent to accommodate his height. He was fully dressed, even his boots were still on, and I noted the dried mud and concrete on them. These were his work boots.

He'd used a small caliber revolver to do the job. The hole in the side of his temple was small, and there were black powder marks around it. The bullet hadn't gone all the way through, so it was still rattling around inside his brain somewhere. I didn't need to take his temperature for an exact time of death. He was still warm, and rigor hadn't started to set in yet. Based on that and the time Kendra had gotten the 911 call, I knew Carl had been dead for less than an hour.

All in all, it was a neat scene. There wasn't a lot of blood. Except for the hole in his head, it just looked as if he were sleeping. I picked up the hand that hung down over the side of the tub and examined it closely, and then I took a swab for gunshot residue and put it in an evidence bag. I'd be able to look at the particles from his hand and clothes under the microscope when I got him back to the lab.

I left the shell casing and weapon for Martinez to document and photograph, and just as I stood, I heard the sound of footsteps coming down the hall.

"Yo, Doc," Martinez said.

"Yo, yourself," I told him. "Not much left for me to do here. He's definitely dead. And he was neat with it. I'll get out of your way so you can document."

"Sheriff's in the kitchen trying to talk to the husband. We got the financials in for Carl and Robert not too long ago. Nothing looks out of the ordinary. Carl makes a damned good living. Robert makes about half his salary, but it's not terrible. Looks like they bought a lake house a couple years back and are making payments on that. But I'd say it's normal expenses for people with their level of income."

"You tell Jack?" I asked.

"Not yet. I emailed everything to him."

I left Martinez to do his job and made my way back to the kitchen. Katie was at the stove, pouring hot water from a kettle into a big mug. I watched her steep the tea and put a healthy shot of whiskey in it.

"For his nerves," she whispered as I came through.

Jack and Robert were sitting at the kitchen table, much like they had the day before. Once Katie had set the hot mug in front of Robert, Jack said, "Would you mind finding Officer Chen and giving her your statement? She's outside with the others."

"Sure," Katie said and left.

I took the seat next to Jack. Robert was shaking and his teeth were chattering. Shock would do that to a person. I physically put his hands around his mug and held them there until he could do so himself.

"Robert," Jack said. "I know this is very difficult, but I need you to talk to me right now. I need to know exactly what happened. Just tell me about your day, up to the time that you got home."

He gripped his mug a little tighter, but didn't drink. "We're hosting a luncheon tomorrow. Nothing big. Just a few friends over for the afternoon." He shrugged and tried taking a sip of his tea. I'm not sure the whiskey Katie put in even registered. "It's just a normal Friday. I kissed him goodbye when he left for work a little after five. He was running late this morning because the timer on the coffeemaker didn't go off like it was supposed to so he had to wait for the pot to brew. I headed over and met the running club after he left. I did three miles." His voice quivered at the end and he took another sip.

"Take your time," I told him.

He nodded and took another sip and then breathed in deeply, steadying himself. "I came back after my run and showered and dressed for the day. That was about eight o'clock. By eight-thirty, I was at my desk in the office working. I stopped around ten and went to do some errands. I stopped by the post office. When I came out of the post office, I got a call from Carl saying there was a warrant to look at our bank accounts and records because Rosie had left Carl her house.

"I was so upset about that," he confessed. "It seemed like such an invasion of privacy. But Carl told me it was no big deal and that y'all just had to look because it was part of the process. Once you looked, then you could eliminate us off the list and move on to finding who really killed her."

"That's right," Jack said.

Robert nodded. "Carl was always right about stuff like that. He was good at being logical about things. After he called, I drove through Starbucks to get a latte, and then I headed to the grocery store from there. Like I said, we've got a garden luncheon scheduled for tomorrow and I was going to make a peach sangria and tea sandwiches.

"When I drove down the street, I got this feeling that something was wrong, you know? People were out in their yards, and they were looking toward our house. When I pulled in the driveway, I saw Edna and Frank outside, which is really weird because we rarely see them, even though they live next door."

"No one said anything?" I asked.

"I asked JoAnn why everyone was standing around, and she said they heard a gunshot. Everyone was trying to figure out where it came from. I told her it was probably someone out messing around in the woods, but she said no and that it sounded real close. She said they called the police. I told her it was probably nothing and popped the trunk to start grabbing bags.

"But I noticed the smell as soon as I walked in the door. That's when I started to get that tightness in my chest. Carl was supposed to be at work. No one was supposed to be home, but I saw his truck in the driveway, and I thought maybe he came home early to surprise me. I put the bags on the counter and I just started walking. I don't know what I expected to find." His breath started to hitch again and he put his cup down when his hands started shaking. "And then I found him in the bathroom."

"Did you touch him?" I asked.

He shook his head no. "I couldn't. I could see he was already gone. I just turned around and went back outside. I think my face must have said it all because Katie came up to give me a hug and I just fell apart."

"Do you have someone you can stay with for a little while so we can finish up?" he asked. "Maybe Katie?"

"It's almost time for Callie's nap, and Katie needs her rest too. I think the baby is going to come early. I'll see if I can go to Janet's. She has the biggest bar, and I could use a sedative."

"Let me talk to her," Jack said, getting up from the table.

"This doesn't feel real," Robert said once Jack had left.

"No," I agreed. And I knew it wouldn't. He was in a state of numbness, but it wouldn't last forever. There would come a time when the reality would set in and the real grief would start.

"I don't know what to do," he said. "What arrangements to make. I need to call his mother. His family. I really don't want to do that."

I took his hand just like I would if I were at the funeral home, helping a widow or widower make the final resting decisions for their spouse. "Make the calls and get it done," I advised him. "Waiting won't make it easier. As far as arrangements, we'll help you with all of that."

"Right," he said, letting out a breath. "You're going to take him?"

"I am. I've got to do an autopsy. But when I'm finished, I'll release the body to you. That's when you can decide what you want to do."

"Carl wanted to be cremated. We both do. It's in our estate papers that we're both to be cremated if something were to happen to either of us. We feel it's unnecessary to pollute the ground."

"Whatever he wanted is what we'll do," I told him.

Jack came back in and nodded to me and I said to Robert,

"It's time to go to Janet's now. Call your family and then lay down on the couch and rest for a little while. You're going to need your energy."

He nodded and half stumbled his way out of the kitchen. I wasn't sure if lethargy from the grief was setting in or if it was because of the whiskey.

"Who called it in?" I asked when Jack came back.

"Edna Bright," he said. "Let's see if we can find a note. What did you think when you looked at the body?"

"It looks like a suicide," I said. "There are powder marks around the entry wound. Enough so I'd say the barrel was pressed directly to the temple at impact. And there's gunpowder residue on his right hand. But I've got questions."

Jack snorted. "When do you not have questions? What about?"

"Just the fact that he came home from work in the middle of the day to kill himself. Why come home? Why not do it in his truck or his office? He's still fully dressed. He's even wearing his work boots. This place is pristine, so I can't imagine him tracking them through the house and dirtying up the floors."

We checked in with Martinez and then moved farther down the hall to an office area. This must have been Robert's space. There was a large desktop with the screen still on, and there were a stack of files sitting next to it. It was a small room that was comfortable in its coziness. I guess if you worked from home, being comfortable was probably a priority.

We moved around the room quickly, but there were no notes, nothing in the trashcans, and nothing indicating Carl had been in the room. We moved across the hall to the master bedroom with the same result. But in the bathroom, I found what I was looking for.

"Bingo," I said, unfolding a crumpled piece of paper from the trashcan. I scanned the note quickly, my brows raising in surprise, and then I handed it to Jack.

"As far as confessions go, it seems pretty convincing," Jack said.

Carl had addressed the note to Robert.

*Dear Robert,*

*I'm not strong enough to live this lie, and I feel this is my only way out. I killed Rosie. It was an accident. I swear. She knew I was having an affair. She'd seen us together, and I knew in my heart she was going to tell you. I couldn't let her do that. You're the light of my life and I'd do anything to protect you. Which is why I'm saving you the trouble of having to see me go to trial and eventually prison. I'm not cut out for that life, and it would be a financial strain on you. As it stands, you have this house and plenty in the bank to be comfortable. Please believe me when I say I'm only thinking of you. I don't know if you can forgive me, but I beg that you do. I love you always."*

"So my dad was right," I said. "The man across the street *was* having an affair with the woman next door to the vacant house."

"Abby Clearwater lives next door," Jack said.

"I guess Harrison Taylor wasn't the only one tempted by her beauty."

When we finally got back to the kitchen to search, I was itching to get back to the body. I don't know why I opened the kitchen trashcan. Maybe out of habit. But I did and used the flashlight I kept in my bag to look down in it. I was lucky I'd had my flashlight, otherwise I would've had a hell of a surprise when my hand grasped at the open syringe laying on the bottom.

"What in the world?" I asked, holding up the syringe.

"Careful with that," Jack said, taking it from me and putting it in an evidence container.

I pulled the entire bag from the trashcan and moved to the counter so I could spread everything else. It was better than taking the chance of getting another potentially dangerous surprise. There were no notes. Just breakfast trash and some junk mail. But there was also a small glass vial, smaller than my pinkie finger.

"It's ketamine," I said.

"Special K?" Jack asked, taking the vial. "I'm not seeing either of them as users. And this doesn't look like what you get off the street. Maybe Carl was nervous about pulling the trigger and decided he needed a little help relaxing."

"This is more than a little help," I said, holding up the empty vial. "I'm glad we found this. It never would've shown up in the tox screen. But now that I know what I'm looking for I can see if there's anything in his system. Ketamine will usually trigger a false PCP reading. And now I know to look for the injection site. If he injected this much ketamine into his body, he would've been out within a few seconds. That's a hefty dose. And he wouldn't have been able to pull the trigger at all."

"Which means someone would've had to help him get those powder marks on his hand."

"Have Chen do a swab of everyone who was home at the time of the shooting," I said. "The best thing I can do is get him back to the lab and open him up. That's where all our answers will be."

# 15

When I came back outside with the body, Floyd Parker was standing there with his camera, blocking the sidewalk so we couldn't get the gurney past him to the Suburban. I wasn't in the mood to deal with Floyd. I'd been learning to deal with my anger from my past, but after seeing my father that morning and seeing the promising life of a man like Carl Planter flushed down the toilet, I was at my boiling point.

"You're blocking the way, Floyd," I said, coming to a stop in front of him.

Floyd had played college ball more than a decade ago and was one of those men who had the kind of neck that just kind of melted into the rest of his body. He'd had muscles and a brain, and he'd been a sympathetic ear one night when I'd had too much to drink and was just a little too homesick. I'd regretted that one night immediately, but he'd never let me forget it. Let's just say I was more of an experiment for him than a one-night-stand, and he hadn't been kind. When my parents had driven their car over the cliff and the FBI had started sniffing around, he *really* hadn't been kind.

My body blocked the gurney and he was trying to move around me to get a shot.

"The public has a right to know, Jaye," he said, smirking. "This is the second body in as many days. Maybe it's time for a change in our law enforcement leadership if this is what Bloody Mary is turning into."

"I know you don't understand the meaning of the word *victim*," I said slowly, "but I have one on this gurney who deserves my time and attention. Get. Out. Of. My. Way."

He dropped his voice down so I was the only one who could hear him. "All I see is a homo who couldn't live with his choices."

I shoved my medical bag directly into his crotch, and while he was bent over, gasping for air, my palm connected with his nose. It gave me great satisfaction to see the blood spattering on his golf shirt. He must've been as surprised as everyone else standing around, because I very gently pushed him to the side and he went. Sheldon and I rolled the body past him and into the Suburban without any other issues, but if looks could have killed, I'd be six feet under. I could still feel Floyd's glare as we pulled away.

"That was intense," Sheldon said, wiping his forehead with a rag. "I can't believe you did that. He was bleeding. Do you think you'll get in trouble? I can run the funeral home while you're in jail."

"I appreciate the offer, but I'm not worried about going to

jail." I had much more important things to worry about. Like getting sued.

"I guess that would make things pretty awkward at home if Jack had to arrest you."

"He was impeding an investigation," I said. "I asked him to move politely and he refused to do so. I have more authority as coroner than you might think. I can have people arrested, issue subpoenas, and hire my own deputies for my office if I saw fit. I don't have to do that because of my relationship with the sheriff's department, but that's how it works in a lot of counties. Floyd overstepped his bounds. Freedom of the press allows you to be an asshole. It doesn't allow you to get in the way of an investigation."

"You said asshole," Sheldon said, staring at me with his big owl eyes magnified through the lenses of his glasses. "That's a quarter."

I turned toward Sheldon, and the look on my face had him shrinking back against the seat. I opened the console between us and dug around for change. Cars were honking behind me, but I didn't care.

I very deliberately tossed four quarters at Sheldon's chest, each one thudding against his breastbone, and then I said the three words that came to mind as soon as he said the word quarter.

"I've noticed you get like this when you go too long without coffee," he said, gathering up the quarters and dropping them in his shirt pocket.

Fortunately, we'd arrived at the funeral home, and I pulled under the carport. The two of us unloaded the body and got him inside and into the lab. Once we got him on the table and out of the bag, I sent Sheldon off so I could do the autopsy in peace.

I turned on the stereo and then suited up. The written documentation took me the longest. Cataloging every item of clothing and pulling off stray fibers or hairs that would have to be tested. I couldn't do that level of testing in my lab, so I'd have to send it off to the lab in Richmond.

Once I got his clothes off and hanging in the curing cabinet, I worked my way from head to toe, front to back, documenting every mark on the body. I found the needle mark I'd been looking for with the help of the ultraviolet light.

"There we go," I said to Carl. "You had some help with that injection, didn't you?"

The needle mark was located halfway between his neck and shoulder, on his back. He never would've been able to reach that spot on his own. Which meant Carl Planter's suicide had just become a homicide.

A normal autopsy took me two to three hours, and you couldn't get more normal than this one. He was a healthy man in his thirties. He'd taken good care of himself. His heart was good. He would've lived a long and healthy life under other circumstances. He'd eaten a chicken salad sandwich and potato chips for lunch, along with a sweet tea. The bullet I found lodged in his brain was a .22 caliber, consistent with the weapon found at the scene.

All I needed to find now was the drug in his system. If I could get that false positive, then I could add one more nail to the coffin when we finally caught whoever did this.

I put Carl back together while I waited for the drug test, and then I sprayed him down with disinfectant and pulled a sheet over him. I heard the beeps of the control panel on the door, and wondered who was brave enough to come down and interrupt me. I was basically finished, but I found the upset of my dad and Floyd was still bubbling just under the surface.

I let out a breath when I saw Jack appear at the top of the stairs. He stared at me a few seconds and then said, "Is it safe to come in?"

I knew he was taking a chance coming down here at all. Jack was one of the toughest people I'd ever known. He could and had dealt with unimaginable horrors. But the smell of the chemicals I used in the lab made him sick every time. It was mostly the embalming fluid, so I was hoping he would be okay since it had been more than a week since I'd used the chemical. I was so used to it, the unusual smells barely registered anymore.

"You're good," I said. "Just be glad you're not Sheldon."

His lips twitched. "I'm glad for that every day." He came down the stairs and I could see the strain around his eyes. "Sorry I missed your destruction of Floyd. Nice shot to the nose. He bled for a long time."

"That makes me feel a little better," I said. "Did he make your life hell?"

"Nah, I told him under the circumstances, we wouldn't press charges for him impeding an investigation. Chen witnessed it and correlated that he wouldn't get out of the way, thus putting the body in harm's way. He finally left when he realized no one was going to be sympathetic to his injuries."

"You think he'll try to sue?" I asked.

"Maybe, but I wouldn't worry about it. We can always file the charges against him. But I'd stay out of his way if you can. He's got it in for you, and I'd hate to have to try to bury his big ass somewhere in the middle of the night. Anything interesting in the autopsy?"

"You could say that," I said. "I was just about to call you. This is definitely a homicide. Check this out." I turned on the ultraviolet light and moved it to the area just behind the neck and shoulder. The starburst of bruising around the tiny pinprick of the needle mark came into view. "We'll have to take DNA from the needle and send it off for comparison, but this is where the killer inserted the syringe and administered the drug. And they didn't do it easily."

"Carl is pretty tall," Jack said. "I can't think of anyone who could hit this angle while he was standing. Which means he was probably sitting down when they did it. Maybe they called him at work and said there was an emergency of some kind. Maybe it was something to do with Robert. Carl jumps in his car and drives home, meeting whoever it is and inviting them inside. Carl sits down at the kitchen table, just like he did with us, and then they move in behind him, stabbing the syringe into the big muscle of his shoulder."

"They'd have to move pretty quickly with that big of a dose," I told him. "He'd start losing control of his muscles immediately. They'd have to get him up and walk him to the bathroom and into the tub. They might have a few minutes tops before he was completely incapacitated. From there, it wouldn't be hard to wrap his hand around the gun and pull the trigger. Do you know whose gun it is?"

"Robert says it's theirs," Jack said. "Robert said he didn't like having them in the house, but Carl insisted. He'd grown up around guns and was comfortable. Robert opened the safe for us in the bedroom. There were places for three guns. The other two were still there. Robert's timeline works out. We've already checked. He was gone when the gunshot went off, but several neighbors verified him pulling up shortly after since they were all outside."

"No one saw Carl come home? No one saw him with anyone?"

"Janet said she noticed his truck in the driveway when she went in the kitchen to make lunch for her boys. She's working from home today. Frank Bright says he was watching the news and Edna was taking a nap. They apparently had a late night last night of stargazing. The Millers were packing. They're getting ready for a long weekend to go see their grandchildren. JoAnn was about to leave the house. She has a spa appointment because she and Harrison have an event tonight. Katie saw Carl driving down the street, but she said he didn't seem like he was in a hurry. She did wonder why he was home in the middle of the day, but she said she thought maybe he forgot something. No one saw Carl go into the house. No one saw him talking to anyone. This is the most maddening neighborhood I've ever seen. Both times it would have been nice for them to be nosy are the times no one saw anything."

"What about Harrison?" I asked, moving back to the urine sample and test strip I'd collected earlier.

"His secretary says he's in a meeting, but we haven't gotten a chance to confirm yet. JoAnn says he's been gone since this morning."

"Drug test is giving a false positive for PCP," I said, holding up the strip. "That's consistent with ketamine."

I labeled the results and put it with the other evidence I'd collected from Carl Planter. Then I handed everything to Jack and rolled Carl into the freezer.

"Something has been bothering me since I talked to my dad this morning," I said.

"You think?"

"No, I mean about something he said. He said the vacant house was getting a lot of action, and that the woman next door and the man across the street used the house frequently. He could either mean Frank Bright, or he could mean Carl and Robert Planter. Maybe Carl was coming home for an afternoon romp."

"Romp?" Jack asked. "Is that what we're calling it now?"

"Hush," I said. "I'm being serious."

"What if Carl had a suspicion that Robert was cheating and decided to come home early to catch him in the act?"

"So now what?" I asked.

Jack looked at his watch. "Ben will be at the house before too long. I've got too many things rattling around in my head. Let's go home and get something to eat. We're both low on fuel. Then we can decide what's next."

# 16

"If I were ever to adopt anyone," I said as we pulled into the driveway and saw Ben sitting on our front porch, "It would be Ben."

"I'm sure he'd be glad to know he has someone to fall back on if times get hard," Jack said.

"I just mean he's kind of like a puppy. Adorable, and cute, and mostly house trained."

"How come y'all have been married a month and Jaye isn't pregnant yet?" Ben called out after we'd gotten out of the car.

"I take that back about adopting," I said to Jack.

Jack laughed and yelled back to Carver, "Because she bought her birth control pills from a vet who sold them out of the trunk of his car. It's like my Kryptonite."

"I knew Michelle did it on purpose," Carver said. "I've known that woman for five years and she's been pregnant four of them."

"You know you're the one who can control that, right?" Jack asked.

Carver smiled and shrugged. "I know, but I'm kind of irresistible, and sometimes she just attacks me. I think she plans these things."

"Are you going to tell her to stop?" Jack asked.

"Hell no," he said. "Do I look stupid? Don't answer that."

Carver was an average guy—average height, average weight, and average features. His hair was sandy blond, his eyes were green, and he wore tortoiseshell glasses. He had a duffle bag slung over his shoulder and a hard shell briefcase in the other. Jack had once told me for as long as he'd known Carver, he'd never seen him without a girlfriend. Women *loved* Carver.

Carver was brilliant with electronics, and in the briefcase was a super computer of his design. He called it Miranda. I'm not sure why, since his wife's name was Michelle, but Jack told me not to ask, so I hadn't.

Jack unlocked the front door and turned off the alarm, and then he showed Ben to one of the guest rooms on the second floor so he could drop off his bag. When they came back down, Ben was telling some outrageous story and Jack was laughing. For that alone, I would always love Ben. There was a lot of stress that went along with Jack's job. And because of my job, there were many nights we brought work home with us. I needed to do better at making sure we had non-work time when we were at home in the evenings—time where we just held each other on the couch and watched TV or played pool or darts in the game room and drank beer.

But Ben always had some story or other to tell, though I was almost positive they weren't all true. And it was a pleasure to see Jack at ease and the stress he'd been carrying around fall off at the presence of his friend. I followed them into the office so Ben could set Miranda up on the desk.

"I'm sorry, baby," Ben said as he carefully took her out of the padded case. "I know you don't like to be locked up."

"I always expect her to answer him," I whispered to Jack.

"You never know," he whispered back. "Their relationship is not natural."

"She can hear you," Ben said in a sing-song voice.

Miranda wasn't just a laptop. The suitcase itself was part of the computer. He hooked up wires, connecting them, and then plugged it into the wall.

"I'm assuming you invited me for the weekend because you missed me," he said. "But just in case, I'm prepared to put this beauty to work. Things have been rather slow at the office lately. There's so much red tape and bullshit going on in the upper levels of the bureau that the rest of us are finding ourselves without a lot to do."

"We've got an interesting case," Jack said. "Eighty-five-year-old woman was clonked over the head in the early morning hours on Monday, and then subsequently eaten by her cats for a couple of days until her body was found."

"Gross," Carver said, eyes wide.

"There are people all over the place in that neighborhood, even that early in the morning. One of them was leaving for work about that time, and six others met in one of the yards to stretch and go running. No one saw or heard anything. Everyone thinks she's just a sweet old lady who bakes for everyone. She used to be a pretty well-known baker, and when she sold *Rosie's Sweet Shop*, she didn't sell her recipes. Everyone assumed she was hiding her world-famous recipes on her laptop. I forgot to mention that the laptop is nowhere to be found."

"Hold on a sec," Carver said, putting up a hand. "You're telling me your victim is Rosie McGowen? Oh, man. That sucks. My mom used to order every birthday and anniversary cake from her. I've never tasted anything like it. You think someone killed her for her recipes?"

"We thought that might be the case at first. Several of the neighbors mentioned companies had tried to buy them from her in the past. She even had a high tech safe installed in her home to keep her laptop in. But then we checked her financials," Jack said. "I emailed everything to you. She's got a bank account that's been doing nothing but accumulating money over the past several months. I'm not talking about a little bit of money. I'm talking about several million dollars. But we're not sure where the money is coming from. The code that shows up on the bank account isn't one we recognize, and when we did a search for it in the database, nothing came up.

"And all the deposits are from the same place?" Ben asked.

"Yes, and there's no pattern to it. It's different days, different times, different amounts. Sometimes there are several deposits in one day. But there's at least one deposit every day."

"It sounds like Rosie couldn't get away from the

entrepreneurial side of things," Ben said. "If she's selling products online, she could collect money for services in a third-party account, and then she could transfer money directly to her bank account. But several million dollars? That's a hell of a lot of cakes she must have sold."

"I'm not so sure it was cakes," Jack said. "We've got no reason to believe she was running a business like that. I don't think she'd have been able to keep it a secret in that neighborhood. Everyone knows everyone else's business. We think this was something different. Maybe not all together on the up and up."

Carver raised his brows. "Maybe online gambling?"

"One of the neighbors thinks she was a madam, pimping out high-priced call girls. Our vic had a tendency to leave at all hours of the night and not come back until morning. We've run her bills in her regular checking account. There's no rent or utility payments going to any other building or residence but her own. But I have to admit the idea isn't completely without merit."

"Well, someone obviously stole the laptop for a reason," Ben said. "There has to be something valuable on there."

"That's why we're hoping you can help us."

"It's possible I can track her computer if I can get her IP address. That's the truly scary thing about technology nowadays. Someone is always watching, and they know where you are, where to find you, and usually if you're thinking of going somewhere."

"Got it," I said. "So if we need to disappear, don't take our phones or computers with us."

"Phones, computers, watches, GPS, eReaders, digital cameras, stereos, credit cards…if you need to disappear it's a hell of a lot harder than you'd think it would be."

There were two knocks on the front door, and then it opened. We all turned to look and see who it was, and then I remembered it was Friday.

"I brought pizza," Vaughn said as he looked at all of us while we stared back blankly at him.

"Great," Jack said. "I'm starving. Jaye and I didn't get a chance to eat lunch today."

"Am I interrupting?" Vaughn asked. "How's it going, Ben?"

"Not too bad," Carver said. "I get to be here for the weekend instead of neck deep in diapers, so there's that. My wife is at the spa."

"I always said she was a smart woman."

"Wait a second," I said. "You've met Carver's wife?"

"Sure. She had to come pick him up the night of the bachelor party. We figured it was time to call her when he kept looking for his computer to make out with."

"You swore the secret oath," Carver said, looked aggrieved. "You weren't supposed to tell anyone that."

"We were there," Vaughn said. "And it was very disturbing, I might add. And the secret oath doesn't count with Jaye. You know Jack has already told her. It's one of those married people rules."

I looked off into the distance to avoid eye contact with Ben and whistled a little tune. Jack had told me all about the bachelor party.

"Oh, fine," Carver said. "Laugh it up. But I wasn't the only one who had too much to drink that night. And if I could remember any of the embarrassing stuff you guys did, I would spill it in a heartbeat."

"Maybe you should stick to whiskey instead of those lemon drop martinis," Jack said. "Those sugary drinks make you forget your own mother."

I covered my laugh behind my hand, thinking Carver had one too many dings in his man card for the day.

Vaughn came into the office and put down three large boxes of pizza, and I went into the kitchen to grab a beer for everyone. When I came back in, I heard Vaughn ask again if he was interrupting.

"I figured Carver could pay his room and board for the weekend by helping us out with our murders."

"Murders?" Vaughn asked. "As in plural? I thought Carl Planter shot himself."

"That's the impression everyone is under," I said. "The homicide hasn't been made public yet. Someone injected him in the back of the neck with ketamine before they helped him shoot himself."

"Damn, this place is going to hell in a handbasket," Vaughn said.

"How come everyone gets to cuss but me?" I asked.

"Because you're the one who wanted to stop," Jack said.

"Oh, right. Blame it on me."

"Look on the bright side," Vaughn said. "You'll have enough in your quarter jar to take a really nice Christmas vacation."

"Are you staying for the weekend too?" Carver asked. "Is this like a bachelor party replay, but without all the embarrassing stories? When are the others getting here?"

"You ask a lot of questions," I said.

"I like to be informed," he said. "Knowledge is one of my strengths. Though oddly enough, listening is one of my weaknesses. I learned that from my last bureau psych exam."

"I'm here because Jaye and I are going to track down Madam Scandal," Vaughn said. "But now that you're here you can probably do it ten times faster."

"Who's Madam Scandal?" Carver asked. "Is this a TV show? Because I don't get to watch anything unless it has talking animals or those weird, big-headed animated kids who never seem to have any parents. They just run around town making decisions without supervision. It's ridiculous."

"Madam Scandal is like the *TMZ* of King George County," I told him. "Last year, I saw an ad pop up on my Facebook account for *The King George Tattler*, and it had a little intro story about Kurt Studman. Of course, I was instantly hooked because Mr. Studman has been teaching at the high school a long time. Super hot, by the way. Studly Studman is what we called him. He taught government senior year and all the girls had a crush on him. I mean, like, smokin' hot. His muscles rippled every time he wrote on the chalkboard."

"He wasn't that hot," Jack said.

"Yes, he was," Vaughn said, chiming in.

"Anyway, I clicked on the link and it brought me to this website. Very professional looking, but designed to look like you were reading an actual newspaper, but online. And right there on the front page was this expose about Studly Studman," I said. "And it went on to say that he'd pick a senior girl out of every graduation class and they'd have to sign this confidentiality agreement. And then he'd introduce them to the arts of sensual pleasures. And then when they graduated, he'd let them go and pick the next girl. He's been doing this for more than thirty years. He's only in his fifties now."

"And he's still hot," Vaughn said. "He comes into the health store a lot now that he's unemployed."

"I don't know how she did it, but Madam Scandal knew the names of almost every woman in every graduating class. I knew he was showing favoritism to that stupid Vicki Turner. There was no way she got through that class without cheating. She was gorgeous, but I've seen her misspell her own name before. Dumber than a box of hair,"

The guys chuckled and Jack said, "It's probably time to move past it, Jaye. It was a long time ago."

"Yeah, well, I got to the end of the story and there was another story. This one about one of the councilmen. But the story was cut off halfway through, right at the good part, and there was this link telling me if I wanted to read the rest of the story, I could subscribe to the newspaper and get it every week for $19.99. So of course, I clicked on it and signed up. It's been worth every penny."

"That's outrageous," Jack said. "I can't believe you're spending twenty bucks a month on that."

"Worth every penny," I repeated, not blinking.

"Why don't we see if we can find out who's killing people on Foxglove Court, and then maybe Carver can help you figure out who Madam Scandal is."

"I hate it when my parents fight over me like this," Carver said. "If only you would give me a sibling to spread some of the attention around, maybe I wouldn't need a lifetime of therapy."

"I doubt we're the cause of why you need therapy," Jack said dryly. "I can think of many other reasons."

"Before you distract me again," Carter said. "You mentioned Carl Planter. Who is that and why did someone inject him with ketamine?"

"Victim number one's next door neighbor," I said.

"Oh, well that can't be a coincidence," Carver said.

"Right the first time," Jack told him. "He came home from work for some reason, met with someone who gave him a shot of Special K, got him to the tub before his body was completely useless, and put the gun in his hand and helped him pull the trigger."

"Sounds like a hell of a neighborhood," Carver said. "We've been thinking about moving. It might be possible now that there are a couple of vacancies on that street."

"Morbid. And that's saying something for this crowd," I said.

"Not me," Vaughn said. "I don't actually think about dead people all day."

"Then you should have more beer," Jack said. "You're about to see Carver work his magic with Miranda."

"Are you sure you don't need to put them in a room by themselves? Things escalated pretty quickly last time."

"Shut up," Carver said, taking the chair behind the desk. He laced his fingers and cracked his knuckles.

"So the FBI takes time to help out with stuff like this?" Vaughn asked.

"It's more of a favor," Jack said. "We could get the information, eventually. But technology isn't as up to speed as it needs to be to get some of the information. Unfortunately, submitting for a tax increase to fund the department doesn't really go over too well in an election year."

"This is why you play politics instead of me," Vaughn said. "You're much more diplomatic."

"Jack, do you still have that big screen?" Carver asked. "I can connect through Bluetooth and put everything up there."

There was a remote on the wall next to the light switch and Jack grabbed it and hit a combination of buttons. A projector and a screen came down from the ceiling and a blue light shone against the screen. It only took seconds for Carter to have dual screens showing on the wall.

"I'm going through vic one's financials, specifically the

account that's been accumulating money. It's actually a pretty sophisticated setup. It's going through a couple of different dummy accounts, and one of them is offshore, before ending up in her bank account. I'm thinking her plan was to see how long she could get by without paying taxes. Probably for the rest of her life if she was eighty-five."

"I still can't see Mrs. McGowen as someone who sells sex," I said. "Even when I was a kid, she was just a sweet old lady. She liked to hug, and she always smelled like sugar cookies. She wasn't exactly a siren."

"I guess she didn't need to be," Jack said. "She just needed to be a good business woman."

"It'll eventually lead us back to the website where she's selling her products. Or girls," Ben added. "Come on, baby. You can do it. Slow and easy now," he said, stroking the side of the computer."

"You're creeping me out, Carver," I said.

He grinned. "I know. That's only one of the added benefits."

I rolled my eyes. "Does anyone need another beer?"

"I do," Vaughn said.

"I'll switch to water," Jack said.

"Carver?" I asked. "I think we have some wine coolers."

The others laughed and Ben shot me the finger, chuckling as he went back to the computer. I needed some time to think, away from the others, so I headed to the kitchen to get the drink refills. I couldn't trust my dad. And I also knew he wouldn't give up on getting those flash drives. I needed to know what was on them, maybe more than he needed them.

The evidence of what he'd done was irrefutable. He'd admitted as much. He'd said he was just a soldier, doing the job he'd been hired to do. But who'd hired him? The CIA? The FBI? Or maybe some foreign government who was paying for American secrets. The flash drives were his insurance policy. As long as he was alive and had them in his possession, he was a threat. Which meant Malachi Graves was a threat to everyone he involved in his crimes. Including me and Jack by default.

I'd always loved the windows in this house, but suddenly, I felt very vulnerable standing in front of the bank of windows in the kitchen, looking out into the darkness. Was he watching me now? And still, the child in me wondered if he loved me, or if I was as expendable as so many other lives had been.

"You tempted me with the wine cooler," Carver said, coming into the kitchen. My head snapped around in surprise, and he held up his hands in surrender. "Don't shoot."

I let out a breath and shook the fog from my head. "Sorry," I told him. "I get lost looking outside sometimes. The darkness has a tendency to suck you in."

"Wow," he said, brows raised. "That's a hell of a picture. I think I'll sleep with my curtains closed tonight. Miranda needs a few minutes of alone time to finish her search. I was kidding about the wine cooler, by the way. A beer is fine."

I nodded, the half-smile on my face somewhat frozen, and I

went to the fridge to get everyone's drinks. I wasn't sure whether to bring up the flash drives. They'd been in Carver's possession for weeks.

"Your face is easy to read, you know?" he said. "They train us to be able to do that in the bureau. Just in case you were ever planning to play poker with me."

"I've always been a terrible player," I told him. "I finally had to marry Jack so he'd stop taking all my money. But it's nice to know he's not the only one who can read my every thought."

He came over to the island and pulled out one of the barstools, taking a seat. I was guessing he had something to say, so I popped the cap on his beer and handed it to him.

"I've known Jack a long time," he said, taking a drink. "Did he ever tell you how we met?"

"Not really," I said, deciding to switch to water too. The stress of the day had given me a pounding headache. "Just that you were in a task force together."

"That's true. It was more than ten years ago. You ever heard of Domingo Garza?" he asked.

"Doesn't ring a bell."

"It wouldn't unless you were familiar with the Colombian drug trade. But the task force was put together to bring down Garza. We knew who worked for him, big players and small players, but we let them do their thing so we could cut off the head. Only we couldn't figure out how they were organizing their drops. It was a pretty sophisticated code, similar to the cipher systems they had in place during World War II. That's why they put me on the team," he said, smiling sheepishly. "I was the code breaker."

"You get to carry a gun," I said, trying to be encouraging.

"Yes, but you really don't want me to shoot it unless I have my glasses on."

"Good to know."

"Anyway, things went sideways, as they sometimes do, and they'd piggybacked a tracer on top of the one I'd put on them. All of a sudden I was sitting right in the middle of a shit storm with a gun to my head and a bunch of very pissed off Colombians trying to carve little pieces off my body so I'd spill names of agents working undercover in their organization."

Carver unbuttoned the top couple of buttons on his shirt and spread it open. A thatch work of raised scars lay across his chest. Then he pushed up his sleeves and there were similar marks there.

My lungs burned, and I realized I'd been holding my breath as I imagined the horrors he must have gone through. I knew the kinds of tools that would make those marks, and none of them would've been pleasant.

"I don't remember much beyond the pain, except near the end, when I thought I was going to die, I remember the cavalry coming in. A big bruiser of a guy in all black with his weapon held steady was all I could focus on." He smiled, his eyes in that faraway place as he remembered the details. "And then someone pulled me up from the chair and held me in front of their body, a gun to my head.

"It was a hell of a spot to be in. For both of us. And I never actually expected to make it out of that situation alive. It seemed like we stood there in that standoff for hours, but it was seconds at best."

"What did Jack do?" I asked.

Carver smiled and finally looked at me. "He shot me."

"What?" I said, unable to contain my surprise.

"Oh, yeah. Right here," he said, pointing to his upper arm. "The bullet went right through me and straight into the heart of the guy behind me. Of course, I dropped to the ground like a stone. But I was alive. Hurt like a bitch though."

"He shot you," I said. "And now you're friends. Men are so weird."

"Hey, once I was in the hospital and all patched up I completely understood why he made the choice he did. It's not a choice I would've been able to make. That's why I work behind a computer and not in the field. And I respect Jack all the more for being able to make those choices. I trust him with my life, and I'd never betray him. Not even for the bureau. With all that said, and everything between us, he still hasn't told me what's on those flash drives."

My mouth dropped open in surprise and I hurriedly took a drink of water to cover it.

"But I can guess, because I am brilliant and what I lack in the field I more than make up for in other areas."

I had a choice to make. If Jack trusted Ben with his life, and he did, then I could trust Ben with my life.

"My father is alive," I said.

Carver choked on his beer, and tiny droplets splattered onto the countertop. I grabbed a washrag while he pounded on his chest and tried to catch his breath.

"Believe me, that's exactly how I feel every time he shows up unexpectedly."

"He's here? In Bloody Mary?"

"For now. Until he gets what he wants."

"The flash drives," he said, knowingly.

"Have you been able to see what's on the drives?" I asked. "Even a glimpse of what's past the encryption?"

"It's a delicate process," he said, frustration evident. "I'm sure Jack told you I tried downloading the contents onto Miranda. I expected it to maybe have some kind of safeguard on it, but the level of encryption was so advanced that it started infecting Miranda with a virus after twenty seconds. If I hadn't shut it down, it would've destroyed her completely. As it was, it took me almost three weeks to get her cleaned up and fully functioning again. I'm working on a few things to get past the encryption. I brought the flash drives with me. We can give it another shot when you guys aren't neck deep in murders."

The pounding behind my eyes had increased and I moved to the cabinet to get some Excedrin.

"I don't understand any of this," Carver said. "Your dad is dead. They found his body. The FBI matched his dental records. Your mom's too. They don't make mistakes like that."

"No, he's just that much better," I said. "And I hate him for it." It felt strange to admit it. How could I wonder if he still loved me and hate him at the same time? None of it made sense. "I've tried to put that chapter of my life behind me. The pain and embarrassment. The scrutiny. I've had every part of my life picked apart by the FBI. No stone was left unturned. But I endured it because he was dead, and when all the scrutiny was over, I'd be able to go back to rebuilding my life."

"But he wasn't dead," Carver said.

"No, he wasn't dead. Now he shows up, haunting me whenever he feels like it, yo-yoing back and forth between fatherly concern and threats when I don't do what he wants."

"What is it he wants?"

"To save himself," I said. "I think that's all he's ever wanted. And a man who fears death that much must really worry about what his afterlife is going to look like."

"And your mom?"

I shook my head. "She's gone. Unless he's lying about that, but I don't think he is."

"I'm not sure if you want my advice, such as it is," he said. "But you're a smart woman. You know exactly what your dad is. It's time to let go of the past and move on."

"What if the past doesn't let go of you?"

"It doesn't matter. He'll try to put his shackles around you for as long as you let him. But you have the key to that freedom. All you have to do is let go and let God and the law do the rest."

"What if the law is just as guilty as my father?" I asked him.

"Do you know what's on those drives?" he countered.

"Not exactly. But what are you going to do if it turns out the law is as corrupt as my father?"

"I'll do what I've always done," he said. "The right thing."

I nodded. "You're a good man, Ben."

"Don't tell anyone," he said, smiling. "I've got a reputation to uphold."

"Holy shit!" Vaughn yelled from the other room.

It was such an unusual sound of alarm from him that Carver and I both got to our feet and ran into the office.

Jack and Vaughn stood facing the wall screen, hands on hips as they read the familiar site that was projected onto the big screen.

"Looks like Miranda found her source of origin," Carver said, heading back to the computer.

"It can't be," Vaughn said, shaking his head. The website was just as I'd described it earlier. It was designed to look like a print newspaper. The words *King George Tattler* were typed in large Old English font at the top of the page. And just below it was the story Vaughn and I had read, sitting in the kitchen, just the day before.

"I don't understand," I said, coming up to stand beside Jack.

"Well, it looks like Rosalyn McGowen was a madam after all. Just not *that* kind of madam."

# 17

I THINK WE WERE ALL THUNDERSTRUCK, BECAUSE NO ONE spoke a word for several minutes.

"No wonder she kept her laptop close," I said.

"No wonder someone took it," Jack said. "She's ruined a lot of lives over the last six months. And she's poised to ruin more. Whoever killed her has likely been a victim of her reporting."

"Or they're going to be a victim," Carver said. "Maybe someone killed her so she wouldn't print whatever she caught them doing."

"Can you do a crosscheck from the people in the neighborhood to the people she's written about in her column?" Jack asked.

"Sure, Miranda can do anything," Carver said. "Except sleep with me. My wife put her foot down about that."

"So much therapy," I said, shaking my head.

"Crosscheck coming up," Carver said.

We waited for several minutes while Miranda hummed in the background.

"I just don't understand how she could've pulled something off of this magnitude," I said. "She's eighty-five years old. The technology alone should be her downfall. Jack's mom still has a flip phone because a smart phone stressed her out and made her cry."

"I'm sure Rosalyn had someone help her set it up," Jack said. "Certainly the dummy accounts and offshore account. I can circle back with the attorney I got her will from. He's out of a high-priced firm in D.C. But with as much money as she had, she would've been able to hire attorneys or whoever she needed to set things up for her and see to her estate when she was gone. It all adds up though. The timeline, the amount of deposits based on what she charges for her subscription service, and the way she kept that laptop locked up as if it were gold bullion."

"It was gold bullion," I said. "Certainly a lot more valuable than recipes."

"I've got no matches," Carver said. "None of the neighbors are listed in any of her articles."

"Damn," Jack said. "But someone knew. These people know everything about each other. They even know about affairs that those involved in think are secret. And they're all great at keeping secrets for each other, but sooner or later details and inconsistencies come out.

"They knew Rosalyn was leaving at all hours of the day and night. She's well known all over the county. Think of how many people's lives she's influenced. Someone is sick, she brings them a dessert, and then maybe they share something with her about their health. Or she overhears private conversations. She's welcome everywhere—hospitals, the courthouse, and everywhere in between. Who's going to notice a little old lady who's been a fixture in King George for more than sixty years?"

"The camera," I said, remembering the digital camera we'd taken out of the safe that morning. "What was on the camera?"

"I'd assigned it to Martinez, but he had his hands full doing the backgrounds on everyone. I told him to just email me the file and I'd go through it."

"I still can't believe she'd print that about us in the paper," I said, my brain finally reconciling the fact that Mrs. McGowen had been spying on us in the back of Jack's unit that night. Of course, she hadn't known it was me, but she should've known better. "It's creepy. What was she doing? Just sitting in her car watching us?"

"For all you know, she had her face pressed against the window," Jack said. "We were both a little preoccupied."

"TMI," Carver said. "Y'all are making me and Miranda uncomfortable."

"Can you imagine the things she's probably seen in this town?" Vaughn asked. "You've got to hand it to her. It's pretty ingenious. Sneaky old lady. And who's going to question her? Plus, she made a ton of money."

"Because of the victims of her cruelty," I said.

"Hey, I'm on your side. Remember how we were meeting

here tonight so we could shut her down? It looks like we weren't the only ones who had that idea. She's gotten hold of some very sensitive information. She's affected elections, real estate developments, and broken up marriages."

"I don't understand why the neighbor was killed," Carver said. "Unless he knew who she was and someone was covering all the tracks."

"I don't know if he knew her identity," Jack said. "I doubt it. But he was one of her beneficiaries. Maybe her killer, and his, thought if Carl was close enough to leave a house to then he was close enough to tell her secrets to. Or maybe they were afraid he'd discover something after he inherited the house."

"Carl was a good guy," Vaughn said. "I don't know Robert well, but Carl would come into the shop sometimes if he was rehabbing a house. His business was very profitable. He wouldn't have needed the added income from Rosalyn's house."

"Maybe Robert needed the extra income," I said. "He's the homebody type. But he seems to have a lot of varied interests. Maybe gambling is one of them, and he just got in over his head."

Jack looked at his phone. "Martinez has started sending the in-depth background reports, so if Robert has a money problem, we'll find it. Carver, I forwarded the picture file from the digital camera to your Dropbox. It's a pretty big file."

"Already uploading," Carver said. "Wow, that's a lot of pictures. I guess she didn't know how to erase them once she downloaded them to her computer."

“Or maybe she didn’t want to,” I said. “Maybe she liked having any image she wanted handy at any time. Like insurance. Her phone and her computer were taken. All we’ve got left is the camera.”

“Good point,” Jack said.

“I don’t mean to be a downer on this parade,” Vaughn said after Carver started scrolling through the pictures, “But unless your murderers are cats, these pictures aren’t doing a lot of good.”

There were *a lot* of cat pictures.

“Speaking of,” Jack said, “What did you end up doing with her cats?

“I had Tyler collect all their stools and particulates from their hair to send off to the lab. Then I called the vet clinic and they sent someone to get them. I’m assuming they’ve cleaned them up and are looking for new homes for them.”

“Maybe it’s just me, but I wouldn’t be too keen on adopting a cat that ate its previous owner,” Carver said, continuing to scroll through the pictures.

“To be fair, if you die and you have a cat, there’s a good chance it’s going to eat you anyway,” I said.

“Good point.”

“What about the website?” Jack asked Carver. “Does she have an archive? Maybe pictures she didn’t use or articles she hasn’t posted?”

“He’s sexy when he’s in work mode,” Carver said, waggling his eyebrows and making me snort with laughter. “So intense.”

"Shut up, Carver," Jack said, his mouth quirking in a smile.

Carver stroked several keys on the keyboard and the website we'd been looking at unfolded.

"It's a basic website, so once I was able to trace the accounts back to the source, it's nothing to hack in and see what's going on behind the scenes. In fact, I have complete control of it. She's got a hell of a following. She's getting about half a million views per month from her subscribers."

"There's only thirty thousand people in King George County," Jack said.

"That's the power of the internet," Vaughn said. "Now every relative of someone who lives here is subscribed and people who used to live here are reading too. Plus, the people who are just nosy."

Jack went back to the board he'd created the day before and studied the pictures and the layout.

"Richard Selby had easy access to the ketamine that was administered to Carl Planter," Jack said. "That all has to be accounted for and submitted to the DEA when it's prescribed or used. Are those records digital?" he asked Carver.

"Yes, each doctor has a prescription number, and every narcotic that he signs for is labeled with a correlating number so it's assigned to a specific doctor."

"This is where things get fuzzy for me," I said. "What reason does Richard have to kill Carl? And what about Keith Middleton?" I asked. "He was standing out front when we got the call about Carl. That's the first time anyone has gotten a statement from him. What does he know, and what has he seen?"

"He's pretty much a non-issue," Jack said. "And I think that's how he feels in real life too. Chen tried to approach the topic delicately, to get a sense of how much he knew about his wife's relationship with Selby. She asked him a lot of questions about if he knew his wife's schedule or activities since he was gone so much. Chen said the look on his face was the saddest thing you've ever seen.

"He said he knew what Monica was like when they got married. She'd been married before and had cheated on her first husband with Keith. Her first husband was a doctor at the hospital and almost twenty years older than she was. When she started the affair with Keith, she said it was because he was enthusiastic and paid attention to her and he still had hopes and dreams. But I guess that wore off pretty quickly when he started working nights and going to school full-time in the day.

"He knew all about her relationship with Richard. He'd had a camera installed one afternoon while she was at work when he started suspecting. He even knew they were using the vacant house at the end of the street from time to time. He's planning on divorcing her, but he wants to finish school first. He's only got one more semester."

Carver made the hashtag sign with his fingers. "Hashtag marriage goals," he said. "Would he have a reason to kill a little old lady and stage a suicide?"

Jack shook his head. "Nope. Like I said, he's a non-issue.

"Take it back to the core," Carver said. "Who benefits? Money is usually the motivating factor when someone wealthy dies." And then a picture came up on screen that definitely wasn't a cat.

"Yikes," I said.

"Or there's that..." Jack said. "That's definitely a good reason for murder."

In the archives of the website were several photographs that obviously hadn't been published. At least not yet.

"I think it's time to have a neighborhood crime watch meeting," Jack said. He looked at his watch. "And I think the earlier tomorrow, the better."

"I don't know what you have planned," I said. "But I can almost guarantee you that it's going to piss off some people."

Jack smiled. "That's just a side benefit."

---

DAWN ARRIVED MUCH TOO EARLY the next morning. Especially since we'd stayed up too late the night before. But I could feel the anticipation pumping through my blood.

Nash and Cheek had been on duty the night before, and Jack had asked them to go door to door, telling each household that there was a mandatory meeting for the adults the next morning to discuss ways to keep the neighborhood safe in light of the two murders that had occurred that week.

I could tell there was something stewing in Jack's mind. He was good at extrapolating data and putting the puzzle pieces together until everything fit perfectly. Which was why I knew he'd already thought of something that had been plaguing me. My father had been just as much a part of the neighborhood the last weeks as anyone, though a silent neighbor. And if Mrs. McGowen had discovered that he'd been living there, or was alive at all, it would have been primo news to feed to her readers. And Malachi would've done whatever it took to stop her. His only saving grace at the moment was that everyone still thought he was dead.

But there were others on Foxglove Court that had more to lose than Malachi Graves. It was hard for a man to lose something when he'd already lost everything.

Jack had asked Martinez, Chen, Nash, and Cheek to be at the meeting, everyone wearing soft clothes instead of their uniforms. He wanted a non-threatening environment where everyone felt comfortable. That's what he was counting on. A comfortable killer was arrogant. And arrogance led to mistakes.

I was the silent type in the mornings. I did this mostly because my brain wasn't functioning well enough to form complete thoughts. At least not until I'd had a couple of cups of coffee, and even then it was sketchy. Jack, on the other hand, had something to say from the time his eyes opened in the morning. I had no idea what happened during the hours that he slept that could fill him with that many conversation topics, but I could only assume he had a much different sleeping experience than I did.

When Jack's alarm went off, I snuggled a little closer to him. He pulled me in, his chin tucked into my neck, and he held me until the second alarm went off.

"I miss our honeymoon," he said, kissing the top of my head. "We need to take a weekend soon. Just a couple of days, and get out of Bloody Mary. It's too easy to work seven days a week when we're here. I miss the days of laying on the beach for hours and just being lazy."

"You miss having sex morning, noon, and night," I said, squeezing his butt.

"You're right. Maybe I shouldn't run for reelection after all. We don't need the money. And then I could retire and have sex with you whenever I want."

"And what would you do with the other twenty-one hours of the day?"

"Think about having sex with you."

I snorted out a laugh and we wrestled around for a bit. I was thinking we might have time to squeeze in an early morning bout when the alarm went off again.

"We don't have enough time," Jack said, reading my mind. "But I'd love a rain check for this afternoon."

"As long as nobody else dies, I'm yours," I said, rolling out of bed.

"I wonder how many husbands get to hear their wives say that," he called after me as I headed into the bathroom.

Vaughn had left the night before after midnight. The time spent together had done us all good, and I knew it was good for Vaughn. He was still feeling his way in the world, getting used to be alone again, and there was a desperation in him that wanted to cling to the time he spent with those he cared about. I was glad to be part of that select group.

After Carver had heard the plan about the neighborhood meeting, he'd told us to make sure we didn't wake him up leaving the house. He hadn't gotten a full night's sleep since he'd gotten married, and he had no intention of getting up early unless the house was on fire.

"I don't suppose you want to clue me in on what you're hoping to accomplish with this meeting," I said after we'd left the house and were making our way through town. "I saw the same pictures you did. Why not just bring her into the station and interview her there?"

"Because there are too many loose ends. And I'm hoping putting her on the spot will bring it all to the surface."

It felt like it took forever to get to Foxglove Court. Martinez and Nash had each parked their units in front of Mrs. McGowen's house. It was central to the street and everyone would see them there.

Jack parked his unit in front of the vacant house, and then we walked to Tom and Lynette Miller's house at the center of the cul-de-sac. It seemed fitting that this was where the meeting should be, considering it was where they gathered on a monthly basis. I wondered if they'd feel the loss of the two people who were lying dead in my lab.

I could hear the murmur of conversation from the back yard, and I assumed that's where everyone had naturally congregated, so we walked around the side of the house and through the iron gate.

It wasn't hard to spot the cops in the group. They stood together, apart from the others, having their own conversation and drinking the coffee that had been provided by the Millers. There was a table with carafes of coffee and juice, and someone had baked cinnamon rolls that smelled like pure sin.

Katie, and who I assumed was her husband Jeremy, and Robert Planter all sat on a lounger together, eating breakfast and talking softly. Robert looked terrible. Like he hadn't slept since he'd found his husband's body. Katie looked uncomfortable and kept shifting the weight of her belly.

The Millers sat at one of the round tables with the umbrellas, and Harrison and JoAnn Taylor sat with them. JoAnn had a mimosa in her hand and was looking off into the distance, pleasantly buzzed, while her husband talked obnoxiously next to her. Janet and Richard sat in two folding chairs. They were sitting together, but there was a lot of space between them. They didn't even look at each other as they talked to those around them.

Monica sat on one of the loungers alone, and Keith chose to stand rather than sit beside his wife. They didn't talk to each other or anyone else. The Greens and Davises sat on the two wicker loveseats, talking quietly to each other. And Abby Clearwater sat as far away from Harrison Taylor as she could possibly get, which meant she was stuck sitting with Fred and Edna Bright.

It was right at eight o'clock in the morning and already the sun was shining bright. There were no clouds, and by the middle of the day there would be no backyard shade.

Everyone was dressed casually for a Saturday morning, and it was obvious by Harrison and Tom's attire that they were planning to spend the day at the golf course. Jack and I had both opted for jeans. He'd picked a black t-shirt and his

Docksiders, and I picked a three-quarter length baseball style shirt that said *Last Responder* on it. Jack had gotten it for me for Christmas and I loved it. And I found it oddly appropriate for this moment in time.

The conversation stopped as we got closer, and all eyes went to Jack. He had that presence about him that easily commanded others. Harrison barely spared me a glance before turning his smirk to Jack. The bastard.

"I appreciate everyone meeting us here this morning," Jack said, taking a position of authority in front of the group. "Under the circumstances, it seemed it was best to speak to all of you at once. Especially since Carl Planter was murdered."

The gasps were audible and everyone started talking at once. But Harrison Taylor was the loudest. He got to his feet, his Bloody Mary still in his hand.

"That's uncalled for, Lawson." His chest was puffed up and he spoke with as much authority as he could muster, similar to what I imagined he used in the courtroom. "I don't know why you're showboating, but if this is how you're going to handle things I feel it's my duty to act as representative for the group."

"Does the group have a reason to need a representative?" Jack asked. "I'd think everyone, you included, would be more worried about the fact that two murders have taken place on this street within a week. Haven't you wondered who could do such a thing? How someone could get so close without anyone seeing them? I'd think you'd be terrified it could happen to you."

Several people in the group nodded their heads.

"You'd think the police would be able to stop it," Harrison said. "This is supposed to be a safe community. But I think your office is more concerned with harassing innocent people than protecting the neighborhoods."

"Unfortunately, you can never predict when evil strikes. And that's all this was. Pure evil. You can sit down, Harrison. You're not running for reelection right now."

Harrison blustered, wanting to argue, but Jack turned his attention back to the group. I saw JoAnn tug at his hand and finally get him to sit down.

"Two people on this street were murdered. Two people who were well liked and loved. They died on a street full of people who watch out for each other and notice every strange car and delivery van that comes along. How did this happen? It's really an incredible act if you think about it."

"I don't understand," Robert said. "Carl was murdered? Why didn't anyone tell me? All this time I thought he'd taken his life, and I was wracking my brain, trying to figure out why." He choked on a sob, and covered his mouth with his hand, and I could see the anger brewing in his eyes.

Katie rubbed his back and shot us disapproving looks. She was a cop's kid, but she wasn't a cop.

"It didn't make sense," Jack said, "when we started putting all the pieces together. But when you get enough witnesses and enough stories, the real truth starts to come out."

"What are you saying?" Tom Miller asked. "Are you saying you think one of us killed Rosie and Carl?"

Jack nodded. "Yes, that's exactly what I think. We'll work our way backwards and start with Carl, since he's fresh on everyone's mind. Carl was given an injection of ketamine. You're familiar with that, Harrison, being the DA. Also known as Special K on the street. We found the syringe and vial in the trash can. Which is very convenient if you think about it. All of the vials are labeled with a serial number, and any time a doctor uses a narcotic, they have to file it with the DEA. Considering there's only one doctor on the Foxglove Court, we weren't terribly surprised to discover that the vial came from Richard Selby's clinic."

Richard came to his feet in outrage. "What the hell are you talking about? I have every narcotic under lock and key, and I account for everything. My reputation is above reproach."

I watched the faces of the others, seeing a gamut of emotions as he made his impassioned speech. But some weren't as good of actors as others.

"I'm not calling your reputation into question," Jack said, taking the wind out of Richard's sails. "But there's no mistake the vial is registered to your prescription number. So it makes you think, who else had access to your locked up narcotics? It's not only who had access, but who has a dice in this game? Who has something to lose? Or gain?"

Everyone started looking around, and gazes finally settled on Janet Selby.

"This is ridiculous," she said. "I thought we were coming here to learn how to protect ourselves. Not to be accused of murder. Richard is the only one who has a key to his narcotics closet. Not even his assistants have it. Who else could it have been but him?"

"Thanks, Janet," Richard said. "I appreciate the vote of

confidence. I didn't realize my wife was going to throw me under the bus."

"Throw you under the bus?" she asked. "What do you know about being thrown under the bus?" Her face turned cold and haughty, and I realized at that moment that she knew every detail of what her husband had been engaged in. And she was pissed.

"Maybe Carl was killed because of what he knew," she said, glaring daggers at her husband. "Maybe he's got as good of a view from the front of his house as I have from my office window. Maybe he got more than an eyeful. Maybe he wondered how anyone could compete with a blonde half his age? Or maybe he decided to get revenge and see how green the grass in someone else's pasture."

Richard went pale and Janet was shaking with so much rage I was glad she wasn't armed.

"What are you saying?" Richard asked. "Did you have an affair?"

"If you guys don't mind settling your domestic dispute a little later," Jack said, interrupting.

I wondered what he was playing at. Jack was normally very compassionate in the way he dealt with people. But he wasn't sparing anyone any mercy, and I realized even though he was calm and matter of fact on the outside, he was seething on the inside. Jack hated being lied to. And he hated it even more when people thought they could get away with the crime.

"And I appreciate the outrage," Jack continued, "but I'd

like to see a show of hands of anyone who *didn't* know that Richard and Monica were having an affair."

Only one hand went up. It belonged to Katie's husband, Jeremy. "Sorry," she told him. "I thought I told you."

"It wasn't exactly the best kept secret, Richard. Of course your wife was going to find out. But you found another way to get revenge, didn't you, Janet?" Jack asked. "Trying to frame your husband for murder certainly upped the ante."

"That's insane," she said, glaring daggers at Jack.

"Really? Because I'm willing to bet when Detective Martinez serves you with the warrant we obtained this morning that we're going to find that long sleeve shirt you were wearing yesterday in the dirty clothes. You washed the gun powder residue when you helped Carl pull the trigger off your hands before we could test you. But I bet you didn't think to wash it out of your clothes."

Reality started to sink in, and for the first time I could see the panic in her eyes before she stiffened her resolve. She shrugged and tried to bluff her way out of it. "You're just guessing. And while I appreciate the drama, I know you don't have much to go on. I heard you admit as much to one of your officers yesterday. No murder weapon. No computer. No suspects."

Jack smiled and it shriveled her cockiness. "And then there's the note," Jack said, continuing. "When you left Carl's suicide note, confessing to the murder of Rosalyn McGowen, it wrapped things up nice and tidy. You deflected Rosalyn McGowen's murder onto someone else, and you managed to frame your husband for murder at the same time with the ketamine. You put the syringe and vial in the simplest of places to find."

Jack took a dramatic pause and looked at all the faces. "The only reason you'd need someone else to take the heat for Rosalyn McGowen's murder, is if you were her murderer."

Janet chuckled appreciatively. "I appreciate the fact that you watch a lot of CSI, Sheriff, but as I've already told you, and others have confirmed, I have an alibi for the time Roz was killed. In my experience, it's impossible to be two places at one time."

"Not when you're lying," Jack said. "But I'm glad you brought that up. Because that's where things get really interesting. It worked out perfectly that you, Robert, and Abby were able to alibi each other that morning. The problem with that is I went back to read Abby's statement she gave to Detective Martinez and Officer Chen. She ran the first mile with you, but she's training for a half marathon, so she decided to keep going another ten miles since she didn't have to worry about Harrison bothering her."

"I object to that," Harrison said. "I've never bothered that woman in my life."

"Give it a rest, Harrison," Abby said, speaking up. "Everyone on this street knows you're a perv. Just like everyone knew about Richard and Monica."

"So when Abby split off that left Robert and Janet to alibi each other," Jack said. "That makes it easy since the two of you came back early and climbed through Rosalyn McGowen's open window. All you wanted was the computer, right? If you could get the evidence she had on you, then there wouldn't be anything to worry about."

There were still no answers from Janet or Robert, but the others had caught on. You could see them starting to put the pieces of the puzzle together.

"How did you find out who Rosalyn McGowen really was?" Jack asked.

"Why are you doing this, Jack?" Robert pleaded. "I could never hurt anyone. Especially Carl. I loved him. He was my husband."

"He also wouldn't have been too happy to find out you'd been cheating on him," Jack said. "Would he have divorced you? Because that would've messed up your apple cart. You're living the life. Working from home part-time and playing the rest of the time. Joining social clubs and spending money you're not earning, while having a piece on the side. It would've worked out well for both of you with Carl dead. You'd inherit everything, and Janet would get the commission as the listing agent for Rosalyn's house. But the house only went to Carl if he was alive. In the event of his death, it would revert back to the estate. You weren't counting on that one, were you?"

"This is preposterous," Robert said, pleading to the others around him. "I was nowhere near the house when Carl was killed. *If* he was killed. There are dozens of witnesses."

"That's because you're the weak link," Jack said. "That's why you had Janet kill Carl while you were at the store. You don't have the stomach for death. It's also why you weren't the one to hit Mrs. McGowen over the head and let her bleed to death. How did you find out she was Madam Scandal?"

"What?"

"No way!"

"That's crazy."

Voices echoed all around us as the news sunk in. Robert sat up straight, his lips pressed tightly together. I noticed Katie had let go of him and had moved closer to her husband.

Jack raised his hands and the noise died down. "You and Janet think you're pretty smart. As long as the two of you stick together and keep your stories straight, no one can catch you. After all, you took her computer and her phone, so there's no reason to worry you'll end up as one of her feature stories." Jack paused and put his hands on his hips. "Except for the backup camera she kept in her safe. And the fact that she'd already written her next story and scheduled it for a special weekend edition."

Robert opened his mouth to speak, but Harrison cut in. "Robert, I advise you to ask for an attorney at this point. You're under no obligation to address these outrageous claims."

"Oh, Harrison," Jack said, his smile razor thin. "I'm so glad you decided to bring yourself into the conversation. You almost got away with it. But that's what happens when you think you're smarter than everyone else. You make stupid mistakes. Like thinking the three of you could hold it together long enough to commit two murders. Like thinking the three of you could continue as you were and not get caught."

Janet, Robert, and Harrison were all on their feet, and the other cops who'd been lingering in the background slowly changed their position so they surrounded them.

"We have the pictures," Jack said. "In fact, the latest *King George Tattler* was posted about fifteen minutes ago. So believe me, everyone has seen the pictures. You're through, Harrison."

"What pictures?" Richard Selby finally asked. "What's the story?"

"Carl's suicide note was mostly the truth," Jack said. "He wasn't the one having an affair. Robert was. With Janet. But not just with Janet. They had a nice little three-way going. Now Janet, you can correct me if I'm wrong, but I think I'm right based on the sequence of the photographs. I'm guessing the affair originally started with Harrison and Robert, and like many people on the street, they decided the vacant house was a good rendezvous point. But like you said, you've got a great view from your office window. You knew about Richard's affair, so I'm guessing you saw Robert and Harrison and decided to invite yourself to that little party for revenge."

Janet stared back at us, wide-eyed, and shaking her head. I think it was finally starting to get through to her that she wasn't going to get away with anything.

"When Robert and Janet came back early the morning of their run, Harrison was already waiting at Rosalyn's house. We found a couple of partial prints on the outside of the window. Who was stupid enough to not wear gloves?" Jack asked. "I'm betting Harrison had them on, because he's no dummy when it comes to this thing. That way he can claim plausible deniability, and it's your word against his, but no proof. What do you want to bet those partial prints match one of you? Is it worth it to go down by yourself and let Harrison get off? I bet he's the one who bashed her in the head. He's certainly got the temper for it. Why should you go to jail for murder one when he was the one who killed her? I bet we can work something out in a plea deal if you talk to me."

"He was there," Robert said, his face pale. He took a couple of steps to the side, and Martinez changed his stance so he could grab him easily if he tried to run.

"Shut up, Robert," Harrison said through his teeth.

"I want a deal," Robert continued. "I'll tell you everything I know. I didn't kill anyone. I didn't touch a hair on anyone's heads. I was only there for Rosie to get the computer. That's all we were supposed to do. I didn't know that Harrison was going to…"

"Shut up, Robert!" Harrison said, lunging for the other man. People scrambled out of the way as Harrison started throwing punches, and Martinez and Nash waded in to separate them and put them in cuffs. Chen put a pair of cuffs on Janet, who was still sitting in complete and total shock.

When everyone was subdued, Jack turned his attention back to Robert. "What about the computer and her phone?" he asked. "What did you do with them?"

"Does this count for part of the deal?" he asked. "I'm telling you I don't want to go to jail."

"Oh, you're going to go to jail," Jack told him. "You just

won't be there as long as Harrison. Just be glad you're not the DA. They're going to tear him up in that place."

"It's buried in my garden," Robert finally said. "That area with the fresh dirt, where I told you I was going to plant the exotic rosebushes. It's all down there. Plus the frame that was on the side of the bed. That's what Harrison hit her in the head with."

Jack nodded, satisfied. "I appreciate your time this morning," Jack said to the others. "And I'm sorry you all had to go through this. Maybe now you can start to grieve and heal."

No one told us goodbye as we led the procession of killers back to the front of the house.

"Carver's right," I said after we got in the car. "You're sexy when you're working."

Jack grinned and then it turned into laughter. "You ain't seen nothing yet, baby."

# EPILOGUE

## The King George Tattler: Special Edition

*My Loyal Readers,*

*We've been through so much together. This has been a learning experience for me, and I won't lie, I've enjoyed it immensely. Some of you might disagree with me, and say that I shouldn't find pleasure in other's suffering. But sometimes people deserve to suffer, and I think we can all agree most of the people who've made an appearance in the KGT have deserved to suffer.*

*With that said, this will be my last edition. There's been a lot of interest of late in finding out who I am. I've found it's a little harder to go out and get the information you seek, and at my age, it's not worth the hassle. There are those who would harm me if they could, but I feel I'm clever enough to let the Lord take me the natural way. I also have enough common sense to shut things down while I'm at the top of my game.*

*So I leave you with a final story that will hopefully bring many women the peace they've never found around this man. To the women who never had the chance to say no. To the women who were victimized and felt like they had to stay silent.*

*There's no reason to tell you more. A picture is worth a thousand words.*

"Wow," I said, shaking my head in awe. "Those pictures are like a car wreck. I can't help but stare at them. Mrs. McGowen did a great job putting those yellow smiley faces over everyone's private parts though."

Jack snorted out a laugh while he poured pancake batter onto the griddle. We'd been stuck at the station most of the morning and afternoon, and Carver had been gone when we'd finally gotten home, saying he'd decided to do a little exploring but would be back for dinner. It was after six o'clock and we figured he'd come walking in at any time, so Jack had put on his apron and decided breakfast for dinner was the way to go.

"In the end," I said, "she was just trying to do what was best for the community. Sure, she affected elections and embarrassed some people with the other stories that were more fluff pieces, but she made some real change with the things she did."

"She was a kind of vigilante," Jack said. "I'm not saying

I'm not glad Harrison Taylor is in jail. But look what happened to her because of it."

"She was very brave," I said. "I think she knew the risks. And obviously, she was feeling the heat, which was why she'd decided to shut things down. But what did she have to lose? She had no family, and she'd stayed devoted to the love of her life even after his death. She was a devoted wife and a brilliant businesswoman. She served the community for decades. All in all, she lived a good life. I think that's as good of a compliment as anyone can say."

Jack moved the pancakes onto a platter, and then came over to kiss me on the forehead. "I think you're right," he said.

His cell phone rang and he sighed, pulling away from me to see who it was.

"Lawson," he said, answering.

Whoever was speaking on the other end of the line had Jack's full attention. His jaw clenched and the scar on his eyebrow turned white. I could tell he was pissed. And worried.

"We're on our way," he said and hung up.

I was already on my feet and grabbing my bag. "What is it?" I asked.

"Carver's rental car was found over the side of a cliff. A tree stopped him from going all the way into the water."

"Oh, no," I said. "How bad is it?"

"It's bad," Jack said. "There were witnesses that said a black SUV ran him off the road."

I felt my blood go cold. "Malachi," I said.

"When first responders got to the scene, Carver was unconscious and the passenger door was open."

"He took Miranda," I said. "We should've known he'd go to any levels of getting those flash drives back."

"Now we know," Jack said. "I had Carver hand them over to me when he got here last night. But there's no telling what information he can get from Miranda. She's classified. He might not even need the flash drives if he can use classified information to blackmail his way off the most wanted list."

"I can't deal with my father right now," I said, shaking my head. "He can go to hell for all I care. The government can deal with him. As long as he's out of our lives, I don't care what happens to him."

"You really think he's going to be out of our lives as long as he's alive?" Jack asked.

I didn't. But I couldn't voice the words aloud.

"We need to go," I said. "Ben needs us."

Jack grabbed my arm before I could rush out of the house. "You need to prepare yourself," he said. "Prepare yourself that he might only need you."

I stared into Jack's eyes and saw the myriad of emotions there—compassion, hurt, sadness, anger—everything I was feeling. I knew what he was saying.

Ben might not need a surgeon.

He might need a coroner.

## DIRTY MONEY-EXCERPT

**Enjoy an excerpt DIRTY MONEY, the next book in the *New York Times* bestselling series by Liliana Hart. Now available!**

Death was an old friend.

There were those who feared death, who tried to defy it with diets and the newest exercise trends. Or by using creams and serums that erased lines, so the skin-deep lies that faced them in the mirror each morning were more palatable to look at.

I had a different view of death. There was no escaping it, no denying it, and no running from it. In a world more and more divided by race, religion, and politics, it was the one thing everyone could agree upon. Eventually, through no choice of our own, we'd exhale our last breath and that would be that.

I've spent my whole life around death. Even as a child I had a morbid curiosity of the process. Which my therapist says is perfectly normal given that I come from a long line of morticians. I'm thinking the other three thousand residents in Bloody Mary might have a different opinion.

When I was a child, most people stared at me with stricken horror as if I were the Grim Reaper himself. I was…different. Small for my age and gaunt with it. Sunken cheeks, eyes too large for my face, and my head was usually stuck in a book so I wouldn't have to talk to anyone.

But Bloody Mary's cautious fascination with me might have had more to do with the fact that I'd told old Mr. Miller that my parents would see him laid out on their slab when he'd wrongly accused me of stealing a pack of gum from his grocery store. How was I supposed to know he'd drop dead from a heart attack less than a week later? Nevertheless, the incident gave me something of a reputation.

My name is J.J. Graves, and death is my living.

I sat in a hard plastic chair in a small, curtained-off cubicle in the ICU at Augusta General. The beeps from machines were a familiar sound, and the smells of antiseptic overpowered the less pleasant odors of urine, blood, and vomit.

I hunkered down in my chair and crossed my arms under my breasts, wishing I'd thought to bring something more substantial than the thin T-shirt and jeans I'd put on that morning. I didn't miss the numbing cold of the hospital. It was easy to ignore the bone-numbing chill when you were running from patient to patient on a twenty-four-hour shift. Adrenaline and coffee made great internal heaters.

I'd spent several years during my residency going up and down these halls or crashing on a gurney in a dark room when things slowed down. I didn't miss it. I much preferred the dead to the living, but in this case, I was relieved that death had been cheated for another day.

I stood up and stretched, and then checked all of the drip feeds hooked up to Ben Carver's body.

"Your wife is going to be pissed you interrupted her spa weekend," I said in a soft voice. I'd stopped cursing a while back, but pissed was on the list of words I wasn't sure qualified as cursing. I brushed the hair off his forehead. "If you wanted attention there are better ways of going about it. Posting the pictures of you at Jack's bachelor party on social media would be a good start."

There were few people I could call close friends. Part of that was because I'd never felt comfortable trusting others with the dark parts of my life, of which there were many. The other part was because I was a genuinely private person, and if I was honest, I just didn't like people all that much.

I wasn't the kind of person who made life happen. Jack was that kind of person. He came into a room and commanded it. People were drawn to him—paid attention to him. I did my best to blend into any wall I came into contact with. I was an expert at hiding. It still amazed me that we were married.

I could never hide when I worked at the hospital. Patients and families had questions and needed reassurances. But in my lab, in the basement of the funeral home, I could hide for hours. For days. The dead needed me. And in a weird way, I needed them.

I twisted the wedding band on my finger and then leaned

down to kiss Carver on the forehead. "I'm so sorry," I said. "Don't give up. We need you here."

A tear had escaped, and I wiped it away hastily and then wiped my hand on my jeans. I went back to my chair and pulled it up closer to the side of the bed.

Carver was a brilliant analyst for the FBI. I wasn't exactly sure what his official title was, but his security clearance was high, he had connections everywhere, and he worked miracles with computers—specifically, his computer Miranda—which had gone missing at the time of his accident.

He'd been staying with us for the weekend, helping us solve the murder of Rosalyn McGowen, a longtime resident of Bloody Mary who had been ousted as Madam Scandal. She'd been publishing the *King George Tattle* for months, spilling all of the salacious gossip the county had to offer. Which turned out to be quite a bit. But her identity had been discovered and her life ended because of it. It seemed like weeks ago, but it had only been less than twenty-four hours since we'd made the arrests and filed all the reports.

But there was no sense of closure. Not really. My father was still out there somewhere, and he'd haunt me until we tracked him down and put him behind bars where he belonged. Our relationship was…complicated.

I'd been under the impression that my parents had both died after my dad had lost control of his car and gone over a cliff in the Poconos. It hadn't been long after that the FBI had raided my home, looking for every scrap of information they could find on my parents. I'd also had my life put under a microscope and was questioned for days on end. There'd been no time to grieve. It had just been chaos.

Apparently, my parents had been using their funeral home to smuggle all matter of things from overseas. They'd been working under a government contract—though which government was never made clear to me—and soldiers who'd been killed were transported to Bloody Mary, Virginia, for preparation, meaning my parents removed the contraband from inside them, and then shipped them on their way.

Jack and I had found proof of my parents' extracurricular activities in an underground bunker in my backyard. The FBI had missed it in their many searches of the property, and I wish every day that I had too. Inside had been a gold-mine. There'd been boxes of cash and passports, files and flash drives, including a box that had my name on it. Nothing like finding out your parents stole you as a newborn from your biological parents. A couple who were probably fairly normal and didn't kill people. And let's not forget about the remains of the man who had a bullet-sized hole in his forehead. Finding that bunker had not been a good day for me.

And then my dad showed up, back from the dead, and expected me to greet him with…well, to be honest, I don't know how he expected me to greet him. It's not like we'd ever been close. But needless to say, we didn't hug it out.

Unfortunately for my dad, he didn't return from the dead before I'd discovered the bunker and removed the body and files. Unfortunately for me, he's had a lot more practice at being a horrible person, so he was able to steal everything from Jack's safe where it had all been locked up. Our only saving grace had been the handful of flash drives Jack had given to Carver.

Carver had been keeping the information from his superiors. No one could know what we had until we could find out who else was dirty—and that included the FBI. The whole operation was too big for my parents to be the only ones involved.

If I wasn't his daughter, we'd probably all be dead by now. Believe me, I've asked myself more than once why being his daughter kept me alive. Not for some misguided familial connection, that was for sure. But there had to be a reason, and I had a feeling that his patience was running thin. He needed those flash drives, and he needed them now.

I knew it was Malachi who'd been driving the black SUV that had run Carver off the road. My dad wouldn't think or care about the fact that Carver had a wife, three small daughters, and one more on the way. Malachi only cared about himself, his survival, and whom he could manipulate to make things go his way.

The truth was, Carver's chance of survival wasn't all that great. When Jack and I arrived at the scene, Carver was already on a gurney and being precariously lifted up the steep ravine where the car had run off the road. The paramedics said he'd flat lined twice on the way to the hospital.

Carver's skin was as white as the sterile sheets he was lying on, and there was a large white bandage on the side of his sandy blond head. The only thing that had stopped the SUV from going into the Potomac was a tree. Unfortunately, the tree hadn't been very yielding.

Ben's nose was broken from the airbag, and someone had sewn a straight row of stitches into his forehead, closing the jagged gash there. The smooth, somewhat childlike face was going to be scarred forever.

I'd stolen a look at his chart once he'd come out of surgery and been brought into ICU. Other than obvious contusions and abrasions, he'd had some internal bleeding, and a broken rib had punctured his lung, causing it to collapse. His collarbone and leg had been broken in multiple places, and his pelvis had been crushed. The surgeons had gotten Carver stabilized and stopped the bleeding, but he had a lot of surgeries ahead of him. It was going to be a long and painful road to recovery.

My phone buzzed and I dug in my bag until I found it. Jack's face was on the screen, and I didn't hesitate to answer. It had been hours since I'd heard from him.

"Any luck finding the computer?" I asked by way of greeting.

"None," he answered. "But I didn't have much hope. I don't know how, but Malachi knows we gave those flash drives to Ben. He knows the computer was the key to deciphering his encryptions."

"But he didn't know I'd asked for the flash drives back."

"I'm thinking he's got surveillance on the house. He might have listening devices set up as well. I would if I were him."

"Or maybe Carver's accident is the perfect distraction to get us out of the house so he can do another search," I said.

"He won't find them," Jack said. "And the house is being watched while we're gone. Inside and out."

"Where are you?" I asked.

"Down in the parking lot. I just talked to Michelle again and she was able to catch an earlier flight. She should land around two, and I've got a couple of guys going to pick her up and deliver her to the hospital safely. See you in a few."

Jack hung up, and I took a relieved breath. There was something about being a cop's wife that was vastly different from being the best friend or lover of a cop. I'd been all three, and the moment I'd said, "I do," I'd felt the weight of what that meant. I paid extra attention when he dressed in the mornings and strapped on his weapon and badge. I noticed the slightest changes in expression or the way he carried himself if he had a rough day.

And I worried. Worried like I never had in my life. Maybe that was because I'd never had anyone to worry about on such a deep level. Jack had always been my friend, and we'd been through a lot together—including him being shot three times while on a SWAT raid in DC—but we were connected on a level now that I didn't realize was possible for two people to achieve. I'd never known true intimacy or what it meant to become *one* with another person until Jack. But there was a price to pay for that kind of love, and I realized every day that one of us might be taken away from the other. It left a hole inside me I couldn't bear to think about.

Jack had been sheriff of King George County for a handful of years, but just because he was in charge didn't mean he had it easy. The budget and resources were small for a county our size, and his cops didn't get a lot of chances to investigate or see the kinds of things cops in the city did. Not that he was complaining. There were worse problems to have than teenagers partying in the fields, breaking up the occasional barroom brawl, or getting livestock out of the road.

But things had changed in our small, sleepy county over the last year. I used to worry about keeping the funeral home in the black, but I'd had more business than I wanted recently. People had lost their minds. Maybe it was the economy, or politics, or toxins floating in the air. Who knows? But people were shorter of temper, shorter of tolerance, and the vast ways of killing their neighbors seemed to be endless. The increase in violent crime was just one of the many things that bothered Jack, though crime was still low compared to other counties our size.

The truth was, there would always be evil in the world. Just like there would always be good. The battle between the two went back to Adam and Eve, and to think we'd somehow change it thousands of years later was naïve. So it was best to suit up, fight, and protect.

## ABOUT THE AUTHOR

Liliana Hart is a *New York Times*, *USA Today*, and Publisher's Weekly bestselling author of more than sixty titles. After starting her first novel her freshman year of college, she immediately became addicted to writing and knew she'd found what she was meant to do with her life. She has no idea why she majored in music.

Since publishing in June 2011, Liliana has sold more than six-million books. All three of her series have made multiple appearances on the New York Times list.

Liliana can almost always be found at her computer writing, hauling five kids to various activities, or spending time with her husband. She calls Texas home.

If you enjoyed reading *this*, I would appreciate it if you would help others enjoy this book, too.

**Lend it**. This e-book is lending-enabled, so please, share it with a friend.

**Recommend it**. Please help other readers find this book by recommending it to friends, readers' groups and discussion boards.

**Review it**. Please tell other readers why you liked this book by reviewing. If you do write a review, please send me an email at lilianahartauthor@gmail.com, or visit me at http://www.lilianahart.com.


*Connect with me online:*
www.lilianahart.com
lilianahartauthor@gmail.com

facebook.com/LilianaHart
twitter.com/Liliana_Hart
instagram.com/LilianaHart
bookbub.com/authors/liliana-hart

## ALSO BY LILIANA HART

**JJ Graves Mystery Series**

Dirty Little Secrets

A Dirty Shame

Dirty Rotten Scoundrel

Down and Dirty

Dirty Deeds

Dirty Laundry

Dirty Money

**The MacKenzies of Montana**

Dane's Return

Thomas's Vow

Riley's Sanctuary

Cooper's Promise

Grant's Christmas Wish

The MacKenzies Boxset

**MacKenzie Security Series**

Seduction and Sapphires

Shadows and Silk

Secrets and Satin

Sins and Scarlet Lace

Sizzle

Crave

Scorch

MacKenzie Security Omnibus 1

MacKenzie Security Omnibus 2

**Lawmen of Surrender (MacKenzies-1001 Dark Nights)**

1001 Dark Nights: Captured in Surrender

1001 Dark Nights: The Promise of Surrender

1001 Dark Nights: Sweet Surrender

1001 Dark Nights: Dawn of Surrender

**The MacKenzie World** (read in any order)

Trouble Maker

Bullet Proof

Deep Trouble

Delta Rescue

Desire and Ice

Rush

Spies and Stilettos

Wicked Hot

Hot Witness

Avenged

Never Surrender

**Addison Holmes Mystery Series**

Whiskey Rebellion

Whiskey Sour

Whiskey For Breakfast

Whiskey, You're The Devil

Whiskey on the Rocks

Whiskey Tango Foxtrot

Whiskey and Gunpowder

**The Gravediggers**

The Darkest Corner

Gone to Dust

Say No More

**Stand Alone Titles**

Breath of Fire

Kill Shot

Catch Me If You Can

All About Eve

Paradise Disguised

Island Home

The Witching Hour

**Books by Liliana Hart and Scott Silverii**

**The Harley and Davidson Mystery Series**

The Farmer's Slaughter

A Tisket a Casket

I Saw Mommy Killing Santa Claus

Get Your Murder Running

Deceased and Desist

Malice In Wonderland

Tequila Mockingbird

Gone With the Sin

Made in the USA
Coppell, TX
31 July 2020